DALTONS DEMON

By
Lisa Jane Holman

Copyright © 2024 Lisa Jane Holman

All rights reserved.

ISBN: 9798324984236
Imprint: Independently published

Thank you to my wonderful husband,
whom has been a great support to me, whilst I spent every evening writing this novel.

Also thanks to my wonderful friends Tash, Amie, Karin and Narva,
for the support that they provided, and the constant phone calls that I subjected them too.

Some phrases or words throughout this novel are written in Spanish.

You will find a handy translation page at the very back of this novel.

ONE

I am startled awake by the sound of glass breaking. I lay as still as possible in my bed, looking around the room that I call my sanctuary. Taking shallow breaths, I carefully sit up, trying my hardest not to make any sudden movements, listening for any tell tale noises that I do indeed have an intruder in my home.

Nothing; no sound, except for that of my heart hammering in my chest and pounding in my ears, I am on full alert, my senses are heightened at the prospect of imminent danger. I sit here, for what seems like an age, but in actual fact it has probably only been a few minutes.

Eloise, you idiot, you're hearing things again, I tell myself settling back down, forcing the covers underneath my chin like a security blanket, trying to get comfortable enough to fall back to sleep. Then I hear it; the definitive creak of the floorboards outside my bedroom door. Too late I hear them, before my door is swung open with a crash, hitting the chest of drawers placed behind it. The impact causing a picture to fall, and knocks the vase, which smashes on the floor.

'There's the bitch! Grab her, but don't mark that delectable body!' The dismembered voice, coming from the darkness of the hall, barks his orders to his minions.

The light in my room is switched on, causing me to blink rapidly, whilst accustoming myself to the brightness, as four of his minions enter my room; to look at them all together, you would be forgiven for thinking that they were straight out of a military training camp, all with a similar stocky build, and crew cut hair, three of them are taller than me but not as tall as the fourth one, or the one in charge. The fourth minion scares me the most, he has short blonde hair, a stark contrast to his accomplices, with black eyes that resemble a black hole, he has a deep scar running from above his right eye to his chin, his face is covered in acne scarred pock marks. When he looks in my direction, I cannot help but shiver. The three minions approaching me, I clutch the covers even tighter around myself. They try to grab my arms, and pin me to the bed, whilst I am trying my hardest to fight them off. My arms and legs are thrashing about furiously, and my right fist manages to make contact with the jaw of the smallest minion, this only angers him, as he manages to get hold of my wrists and tie my them together tightly with zip ties, I can already feel the plastic digging into my flesh. So now my wrists are bound, and my knuckles hurt like hell from the impact with his jaw, which didn't even make him flinch, he must be pumped full of some form of narcotic. I try to raise the alarm by screaming, as a rag is hastily shoved into my mouth, silencing me. It is pushed so far into my mouth, it hits the back of my throat, I am trying my hardest not to gag; I will not show any sign of weakness to these bastards.

  I am dragged out of the relative safety of my bed, the cool night air hitting my bare flesh, shit I'm naked, why on earth didn't I wear nightclothes? Tonight of all nights!

  I am forced to stand face to face with the man in charge, he stands a good foot above me; at least 6'4', the man I have been tracking for all of this time, but now it's too late, they have found me. How? Someone must have betrayed me, but whom?

'I've been looking forward to meeting you Laura,' oh good, relief fills me as I realise that he doesn't know my true identity, 'or should that be Eloise?' Shit, shit, shit, I have definitely been betrayed. 'After all the trouble you have caused me, I am going to look forward to this.' The smile forming on his lips doesn't quite reach his black, soulless eyes; somehow, I can't help thinking that I am not going to enjoy whatever it is that he has planned for me. How could I have been so stupid? I thought that I had been careful and hidden my tracks, but apparently I must have slipped up somewhere.

'Take her!' he commands with an air of authority.

Before I can compute what is happening, a bag is being placed over my head, covering my eyes and stealing me of my vision; for some reason this makes me even more scared for my future wellbeing. My sense of smell and hearing is becoming heightened, I try to ignore the sound of my heart pounding in my ears, and the images of my cold, lifeless body that are flashing, on repeat, through my mind. I can smell him; expensive cologne does little to mask the smell of him; a mixture of sweat, whiskey and stale tobacco smoke. His minions smell even worse, the combined scents of cheap cologne, sweat and halitosis, this, coupled with the fear I am feeling, make me retch, if it wasn't for the gag I swear I would be sick.

He obviously takes my convulsions as a sign of fear, relishing in the effect it creates in me, 'afraid little one? You should be! I've been very busy making plans for you; I have invented a whole new level of debauchery, especially for you! I cannot wait to hear you begging me to stop!'

I try my hardest not to shy away at his words, trying to

keep my fear under control. I have heard, through the grapevine, how he treats the girls in his care; well when I say in his care; I mean trafficked and abused.

'Check the house! Find, and collect, all of the evidence leading back to me, and our operations. Don't forget any hard-drives that may be laying around, when we get back to the compound, get the tech team to check her Internet history and all of the documents as a matter of priority. When you have done that, torch the place, make it look like an accident'

Torch it? Seriously?

'I know what you are thinking little one; that someone will come looking for you.' He's laughing, the son of a bitch is actually laughing! But that laugh? I recognise it, but from where? 'Don't worry; no one will come looking for you. Thanks to an overzealous client, we have the perfect body to put in your place. He likes to break things, especially faces and jaws! If you don't please me, I may have to introduce you to him, he loves a new plaything.'

Now I am scared; my life is on the line, and I have to "please him" to survive. Can I even do this? Despite being 23, I am still a virgin; sure I've had a few quick fumbles with boys, even a couple of girls in college and university, but as for full on penetration? Nope. It isn't because I have been 'saving' myself for the perfect somebody, nothing as out-dated as that, I am just not someone who is comfortable with having one night stands, and being left to suffer the consequences in the morning; I had seen first hand the worry that unwanted pregnancies and STD scares had caused some of my friends; and it wasn't pretty. I just felt that you should be in a loving, and committed, relationship before giving everything you have. In my early years no one had even come close to being relationship material. I could see the boys that showed any signs of interest for what they really were - players. Then, as I got older, I stopped looking for someone who was relationship worthy, consigning myself to my work as an investigative journalist. Although, the predicament I now find myself in, caused me to wish that I had opted for the one-night stands. I could have had a couple of kids by now, surviving only on Child Maintenance and government handouts. At least I would probably be a lot safer than I currently am now.

'Boss, the house is clear and we have all of the hard drives for the tech guys to check when we get back to base. We've rigged the fire to look like a gas leak, we'll be miles away before it goes off, but we should really leave now before we draw any attention from nosy neighbours,' one of the minions tell him.

I am dragged naked out of my room, and forced down the hallway towards the rear door of the kitchen. Unable to see, my bare feet make contact with the broken glass caused by their entrance into my home, I wince and cry out in pain; this damned gag muffling the sound. They chose their entry point well, no one would have seen them come in, as this side of the house is shielded from the road; mind you the whole house is virtually invisible from the road, thanks to the damned 6 foot high conifer hedging surrounding the house. When I initially viewed this house, before purchasing it, I loved the thought of the privacy the hedging offered; my own little piece of heaven on earth.

He must have noticed my reaction to stepping barefoot on broken glass, because in the blink of an eye he had picked me up, barely straining underneath my weight. Not surprising really as at 5' 3', and only weighing about 8 and a half stone, I must have felt like a sparrow to him. Being this close to him repulsed me, I can feel his rock hard muscles beneath his shirt, and the overpowering smell of his expensive cologne is intoxicating. Instinct makes me place my hand on his chest, why on earth did I do that?

I hear the click of a car boot being opened; oh god, are they going to put me in the boot? Like a piece of rubbish? Before I know it, I am unceremoniously dumped on plush leather seats, as I hear a dragging noise coming from the rear of the car.

'We've put Savannah in the bed, no one will be any the wiser, just like last time' a different voice this time.

Wait? What? Last time? They've done this before? I've been on their trail for what, 18 months, maybe even 2 years? I have never found any evidence that they've staged an explosion to cover up a murder! Oh god, I'm dead already, no one will come looking for me if they think that I was in the house when it burned down. My options for escape, or rescue are quickly expiring. But then again, who would bother looking for me? No family and not really any close friends to speak of, only a few acquaintances. The joys of growing up in care, you become shielded from humanity, building a brick wall of security around yourself.

I can't help but feel sorry for Savannah; she would have come to this country hoping for a better life, only to find herself a victim of a monster who beat her to death; wondering if I now faced the same unfortunate fate. I shudder, from the coldness of the feel of leather on my naked body, although if I am honest with myself; the involuntary shuddering is caused mainly from fear.

'Don't worry little one,' he whispers in my ear, 'it won't

be long before I get to punish you for all of the trouble you have caused me. I cannot wait to show you what I am planning, I am getting very excited!' Before I knew what was happening he places my hand on his crotch. I know I am no expert, but in my mind that is huge, and there is no way that it will fit anywhere in my tiny frame. I snatch my hand away as quickly as it is placed there, thankful for the bag over my head that was hiding my embarrassment, which earns me another chuckle. 'Getting shy on me? You certainly weren't shy when you were dancing in my club. I may have to install a pole, so that you can give me a private rendition'

Oh god, I now know who he is; Dalton Mercedes. My boss. Or, if I am to be more accurate, my pseudonym, Lauras boss. Head of the cruellest crime syndicate going - The Shanks.

As an investigative journalist, I have found that it is easier to get to grips with a story if you invent an alternate persona; Laura Elliott, 25, was mine. She came from a small North Devon village and moved to London to chase fame and fortune; she didn't really mind what she had to do to become famous, as long as she was. Things didn't go to plan for poor Laura; facing eviction, she turned to becoming a topless waitress at a seedy underground bar.

After a busy late shift, they were told that the boss, Dalton, was making a rare appearance to interview some new podium and pole dancers. He had requested that all staff stay to simulate a busy club, if the dancers couldn't perform in front of staff, than there is no chance that they could perform in front of the punters. Being naïve, I didn't realise until it was too late that all of the waitresses were expected to audition. There were no other interviewees; just the waitresses. If you refused, or didn't cut the mustard, you were sacked on the spot. I couldn't risk this; I was sure that I was so close to getting the scoop of a lifetime, whilst also bringing down one of the biggest crime syndicates in the City, and hopefully saving some poor women from an awful fate. So I did what every good undercover journalist would do, I danced; I danced like I had never danced before.

Ok, I'll admit it; I'm as scared as hell right now. I can't speak, because of the gag, which has been pushed so far down my throat that I am struggling to breath. I can't see either, because of the bag they put over my head, so all of my senses are heightened; my arse is as cold as hell from the leather seats, my foot is throbbing like you wouldn't believe and I can feel the blood dripping out of the cuts on my sole, I can swear that there are still some shards of broken glass stuck in the open wound.

I can hear the men, if you can call them that, speaking in a foreign language that I cannot place. Dalton is barking out his orders and his minions are obeying, like puppies seeking approval from their master. I am pretty sure that I am alone in the car; after being dumped here I didn't sense the movement of someone else getting inside. A small glimmer of hope as a plan begins to take shape in my mind; I wonder if I can make a run for it?

I am almost sure that Dalton will still be on the side of the car where he put me in. With the escape plan and decision made, because after all I have little to loose right now; putting the least amount of weight on my damaged foot as possible, I try to move to the other side of the car, I am finding it impossible to move as my bare skin has become welded onto the leather seat, I cannot put my wounded foot to the floor for the sheer agony of it, and my hands are tied so tightly that I am beginning to lose the feeling in them. Leaning to one side, I try to detach myself from the seat; success, now the other way; the closed door is too close, impeding my movement to the side, so I cannot completely detach my welded skin from the seat, I wonder if it will work if I roll across the seat, probably not my best idea, I think, as I land with a bump in the foot well. Fuck! Well I am no longer stuck to the seat, but have managed to become wedged in the foot well instead. Testing for leverage with my good foot, and with a lot of manoeuvring, I manage to make it to the other side of the car; fumbling for the door catch, desperate to make my escape before they come back. A huge sense of relief washes over me as my hand makes contact with the chrome handle, which is quickly chased away by fear as I feel the handle give way beneath my touch, I realise that all of my efforts have been in vain as I hear the door being opened from the outside. I can only imagine what I must look like to the person who opened the door, as I fall out of the car, naked and bleeding.

My actions obviously anger him, as I am roughly dragged out of the car and forced to stand upright, I feel a shovel-like hand grasp tightly around my throat, my bound hands reach for the fingers that were cutting off my air supply even further. I was at the point of passing out before hearing, 'try that again Bitch, and you will be very sorry! I may even pass you around to my men when I'm finished with you'

I must have passed out, for I am sure that I would have remembered being placed back in the car, with a seat beat securely fastened around me. I can feel the movement of the car as it speeds off, how long was I out for? The side of my head feels slightly bruised, but I am not sure what could have caused it. Then as we turn a corner, far too quickly, the momentum forces my head to make contact with the car window, so that is why it's sore. I guess that because I am unable to see the road in front of me, I am unable to brace myself going into the corners, the movement causing me to hit my head. If it weren't for the seatbelt holding me in place, I am sure that I would have been thrown around the back of the car as well. I do not know how many men are in the car with me, as I was unconscious then they got in, but I can feel the heat radiating off of the one seated next to me; from his scent I would hazard a guess that it was Dalton.

    'We are five minutes out, is everything prepped and ready to go? I do not want any problems or mistakes this time, do you understand? If there are, I will be less than forgiving' Daltons voice breaks me from my thoughts, as I do not hear a reply, I can only assume that he is talking to someone on the phone. He must have sensed that I was no longer comatose, as I was trying my hardest to stop my head making contact with the car, placing his hand on my knee, he began snaking his fingers slowly up my thigh, 'mmm, I'm going to look forward to ruining you' I clamp my thighs tightly together with all of my strength, trying my hardest to deny him entry to what he so obviously has plans on taking. This does not deter him, chuckling to himself, he forces my legs apart, and starts rubbing my very sensitive part, I had never been touched like this before and I couldn't understand why it felt so good, especially considering the situation that I am currently in. The tyres squeal in complaint, as the car comes to an abrupt halt, and I thank my lucky stars that he is forced to stop his assault on me, I am sure that my body would have started to betray me if he had continued.

Hearing the car doors opening, I can smell fumes and engine oil; there is also a strange whirring noise. I am very tempted to lift up the bag slightly and peek out from underneath it, but pure fear stops me, what was his threat? Oh yes, "passing me around to his men", I am not stupid and I am a fast learner, if I please him enough, and do as he commands, he may just let me go. Yeah Eloise, I think to myself, in your dreams.

I feel a draft of cold air, as my door is opened and I am removed from the car. I can feel a long coat being placed around my shoulders, it is either being used to protect me from the chill in the air or to protect my dignity from prying eyes, I have not yet decided which one.

I am forced to hobble across the smooth tarmac; as the person who is holding me has a much larger gait than mine, and drags me from the car. Someone must have noticed that I was struggling to keep up, I think even on a good day, and without glass in my foot, I would have struggled to keep up. Before I know it, I am thrown over his shoulder in a fireman lift. The movement of this makes the bag covering my head fall away onto the floor, this is when I get the view of my surroundings; we are in a large aircraft hanger, there are four black Mercedes 4x4's, and about a dozen heavily set and heavily armed men, they all have ear pieces in; which leads me to assume that they can only be body guards or some form of security detail. Then I see it; a private jet, it's engines are already warming up, awaiting the boarding of its final passengers; this explains the smell of fuel and oil, and the whirring sound I could hear earlier.

Dalton carries me up the steps of the waiting aircraft; I can tell it is Dalton because of his distinctive smell. Before I know it we have reached the top of the steps, I can't see much from my vantage point, except for the white leather seats on either side of the planes walkway, and a large, fully stocked bar, but it appears to be quite spacious. Dalton takes me to the back of the plane and through a set of double doors. I am thrown down onto what can only be described as a really soft, and really large bed.

Oh god, the look in his eyes, the look of pure lust. How do I get away from this and him? How do I tell him that I am still a virgin? Would he even believe me? I swear the look he is giving me, if I was dressed, I would feel as if he was undressing me with his eyes. I hold my bound hands up, trying to plead with him for mercy; the fear I am feeling is clearly evident in my piercing blue eyes. After all, until tonight I had no clue that he was the person I had been trying to track down for a story, he dipped his cap so to speak.

If he would just take this gag off, I could explain to him that I am no threat, I could plead and bargain with him to let me go and I would swear that I wouldn't tell anyone what had happened tonight, I'd go back to my life and forget all about him, I'd drop the investigation, and dispose of all of the evidence that relates to him. Oh yes, it suddenly struck me; I have no life to go back to, they saw to that when they torched my home, and left the body of poor Savannah in my place; everyone who knew me will think that I am dead. I have nowhere to go; I am trapped.

I can hear the doors to the aircraft being closed and the engines being revved ready for take off.

There is a faint knock on the door leading to the cabin, 'yes?' Dalton sounds irritable, 'what is it? I told you that I didn't want to be disturbed' Leaving the room he looks back at me, 'there are clothes in the wardrobe, they look about the right size for you, get dressed!'

I look at him, then at my bound hands, err hello, how? Realising that this would be an impossible task with my hands bound, he swiftly removes a pocketknife from his jeans and cuts the ties. Then raising the knife to my face, and with a menacing look in his eyes, he tells me 'try anything, anything at all, and I may have to make your smile wider, do you understand?' I nod frantically, not wishing to be harmed any further than I already have been.

When he leaves, I do my best to remove the gag from my mouth, with hands I can no longer feel, gently rubbing at my sore cheeks and jaw. Catching a glimpse of the damage done to my wrists; I can see the red welts left behind from where the ties were digging into my flesh, I tenderly touch the marks, trying to get an idea of how deep they are. The pain of pins and needles starts to set in, as the blood flow begins to circulate again, I try rubbing them, but this only makes the pain worse. I have no choice but to wait it out, hopefully it won't take long for normal service to resume.

Taking in my surroundings, I notice that this bedroom isn't actually that bad. The bed, in the centre of the room, is large and comfortable, there is a fitted wardrobe and another door leads into the en-suite facilities; which I decide to take advantage of. I check my reflection in the mirror, I look awful; my pink complexion has disappeared, to be replaced with a shade of washed out grey, splashing some cold water on my face, in the hope that it will make some colour reappear, whilst also removing the tear tracks running down my cheeks, stopping at my full pink lips. My piercing blue eyes look sad and worried; it must be true that the eyes are the gateway to the soul. My jet-black hair is no longer in its usual poker straight style; instead it has become all knotted and unruly; as if rebelling at our current situation. I find the sudden compulsion to brush it, needing some form of normality and to take back control on a small part of my life. Rummaging through the drawers and cupboards in the en-suite, I finally find what I am looking for, a small comb. I sit naked on the bed, combing my hair, humming to myself whilst lost in thought, and this is when Dalton walks in, I can't help but freeze in fear.

At first he looks so angry that I have disobeyed him, then his face shifts to that of sadness and pity. He moves stealthily across the room and sits on the bed behind me, taking the comb from my frozen hand and continues to comb my hair. What the hell is going on? He breaks into my home, threatens me, abducts me, hurts me, eradicates my existence and now he's combing my hair? He obviously has some serious issues. Worried that I may anger him in some way, I sit as still as a statue, my heart pounding in my chest, taking shallow breaths, waiting for him to leave, or speak, or anything really. I feel the pressure on the bed behind me move as he gets up, he crosses to the wardrobe and selects some clothes for me to put on.

'Get dressed,' he orders as he places a pair of pants, jeans and a vest top on the bed next to me.

'I can't wear that,' I shrink back at the look on his face, at my blatant refusal to do his bidding, 'my foot is injured, so putting jeans on would be impossible, I am sure that there is some glass stuck in there'

He looks down at my foot as if seeing it for the first time, then throws a dress in my general direction before storming off angrily.

What on earth just happened? He switched from tender to angry in the blink of an eye. He is so volatile; I don't think that I will be able to survive this, physically or mentally.

I have heard, as has everyone, of the phrase "fight or flight" and that you never really know what instinct you have, until you are faced with a life or death situation. Well, I can honestly say that my instincts have been tested tonight, and that I have tried, and failed miserably at both. So what comes next, submission?

Sitting on the edge of the bed, hoping to get an insight into Daltons volatile personality, I try to remember all of the information that I had found out during the course of my investigation. There were various gangs around London that I had looked into, but the rumour mill and Chinese whispers had always distorted the facts, trying to get to the source of each rumour and peel away the exaggerations was a painstaking process. Even now, after years of trying, I am not sure that I have all of the facts, making me read through everything over and over again.

But from what I can remember, the street gang, or the crime syndicate, under Daltons control were nicknamed The Shanks, namely because, at their inception, their weapon of choice were knives. They were easier to conceal and they didn't make a noise unlike guns. You could sneak up on your victim, and inflict injury, whilst passers by were none the wiser.

They rose to power 20 years ago, under the command of Daltons father, Ricardo. Primarily they were small time drug smugglers and dealers, but they were very good at what they did, they tipped off the right people, at the right time and flooded the market with contraband; heroin, cocaine, speed, amphetamines, you name it; they could get it into the country.

They undercut everyone and put plenty of gangs out of business. Word of their methods of torture was passed from gang to gang, making quite a reputation for themselves. Their name was whispered in hushed tones, everyone fearful of retribution. If you were sensible; when The Shanks moved in on your turf, you joined them, moved away, or voluntarily retired, before they could retire you. There was no point in putting up a fight, as people were going missing, left, right and centre, the Police sweeping it under the carpet every time; some through fear and others through the large brown envelopes full of notes, which bought their silence.

Rumour had it that a member of the gang enjoyed mutilation and torture, he got off on inflicting pain on anyone who dared to challenge the Mercedes family. Of course, this is all rumour and hearsay, no bodies, or even bits of bodies have ever been found.

Everything was going well for the family, and before long they were the biggest 'importer' of narcotics globally, at this point it was only narcotics that they dealt in.

They had heard that the trade in dealing in the importation and exploitation of the people was becoming more and more profitable, this was partly due to the amount of people living in poverty, in war torn countries, but they were never interested in pursuing this side of the 'importation' business. That is until one January night when everything changed.

It has been told that Ricardo had returned early from a business trip to Mexico, he found his wife and his 16-year-old son was missing. All of the guards assigned to Margarita and Dalton had been killed. Expecting to be greeted at the door by his loving wife and fun loving son, whilst instead he walked into a massacre!

Ricardo, distraught and out for blood, called in the all of the favours owing from the crime syndicates that were loyal to him, and tasked them with tracking down his family, money was no object, leaving no stone unturned they drove fear into everyone they came across until Dalton and his mother were found.

With his wide influence and connections, it didn't take long. A rival gang had taken them; they had needed a cash injection quickly, and had previously propositioned Ricardo, requesting a large investment from him, in return he would be gifted a sizable share of their trafficking business. Ricardo refused, viewing them as lower than low, and not businessmen at all; little boys trying to play at being big men.

By the time Ricardo had found his wife and son, it was too late, his beloved Margarita had been tortured and raped, before dying from her injuries. Her poor broken body told the tale of the horrors she was forced to endure. Poor Dalton, was found manacled and chained to the wall, in the room next to where his mothers body was found. To protect him, he was never told what had happened to his mother, only that she was no longer with them.

After the death of Margaritta, Ricardo sank into a deep depression, consumed with grief. He began to lose interest in the running of the business, and the family faced loosing everything they had worked so hard to build.

Dalton took it upon himself to take over the running of the firm, even forcibly taking over the trafficking business from his abductors and his mothers murderers. The depression, grief and a rage he had never felt before changed him. Gone was the young man full of fun, his whole life laid out in front of him. His mother was no longer there to shield him from the rage of his father, and the truth behind the family business. After loosing her so violently, and coming to terms with what his world had now become, the demons were quick to take over, and drain him of all feeling and pity; he had lost all of his humanity.

It is strange the tricks that your mind can play on you when your senses are heightened. I have completely lost track of time, we could have been in the air for 5 minutes or for an hour, all I know is that it feels like we are beginning our approach to land. But land where? I raise the blind from the window, trying to get a glimpse of a landmass that I may recognise. I'm shocked to discover that it's daylight outside, I am pretty sure that it was the middle of the night when I was abducted, so we have definitely been in the air for more than 5 minutes, we could have possibly even crossed to a different time zone. When I look out of the small plane window all I can see is ocean, a crystal clear, beautiful blue hue of an ocean, but an ocean none the less. How can we be landing in the ocean? I start to panic, thinking that I am the only one left on the plane and that they mean to crash it with me inside. But I don't remember seeing any parachutes, and I am certain that I would have heard the door being opened, and that I haven't dozed off, enabling them to land, disembark and then set the autopilot on take off.

Then I see it; a speck of an island, which is gradually becoming larger as we approach. I search the surrounding ocean, trying to gauge how far from the mainland it is. All I can see is the ocean; there is nothing else around. Panic starts to set it. I am going to be held prisoner on an island in the middle of nowhere;

at least if we'd stayed in London there would have been a small chance of trying to escape. But here, where could I run too?

I am jolted out of my thoughts as the wheels make contact with the landing strip; a blast of turbulence throws me to the floor, adding even more bruises to my injuries. I can hear the engines squeal in defiance, as the pilot is trying to slow the propulsion of the craft, too quickly for it's liking; it must be a really short runway, but then with the small glimpse I had had of the Island I couldn't understand how it would be possible to land it there anyway.

When the jet finally comes to a stop I try to ease myself off of the floor, without damaging my foot even further. During the flight I looked at the cuts on the sole of my foot and as suspected, there is indeed glass buried inside, even though I had tried my best to remove it, I couldn't, it was just too painful, and I was worried about making it worse, or accelerating the blood loss.

Looking up when someone enters the room, I see the tall blond with a scar running down his cheek. He looks down on me with a look of disgust; out of all of the minions this one scares me the most. Involuntarily, I am scooting back from him trying to make as much distance between us as possible. With one stride he closes the gap between us, grabbing me by the arm and forcing me upwards in one agile move; his grip around my upper arm is so tight I cry in pain, I can feel his fingers digging into my muscles and nerve endings which cause a shooting pain up my arms, I try to move out of his grasp; one, because he scares the living bejesus out of me, and two, I didn't want even more bruises to add to my list of growing injuries. Doing this angers him, and earns me a slap around the face, adding another bruise and split lip to it. Christ he can hit hard; my head is jolted back so fast that I am sure that I now have whiplash on top of it all.

I have always considered myself a strong willed person who knows her own mind, and doesn't back down easily. Always there to fight for someone, whether it is a lost cause or out of the corner they have been forced into; standing up for the small man. But in my current fragile state I find myself subdued, looking only at the floor whilst I am dragged off of the plane and put into another black Mercedes 4x4.

The short walk from the plane to the car, told me that we had indeed crossed time zones, judging by the climate I'd say quite a few. It was hot, but not a clammy hot, like in the UK. The heat at home is stifling, you are sticky with sweat before you know it; especially in the city, where a summer breeze cannot reach the ground between the high rises. It was during the summer that I realised how much I missed the coast, waking up and looking from my lounge window to see the Burrows and the sea beyond, spending my summer days at the beach, swimming, surfing, and sunbathing, there is no better feeling in the world.

Three of the minions who entered my home and abducted me, piled into the car with me, thank god Blondie wasn't one of them, perhaps I could reason with these ones? It has to be worth a shot!

'Where are we?' nothing, no response, not even an acknowledgement that I have spoken.

'Where are you taking me?' Again nothing.

'Look, you don't have to do this. Just let me go. If it's money you want, I have money' well my editor does, but I am almost sure that he would pay my ransom. 'Just turn around, put me on the next plane out of here. I swear I won't tell a soul. You can tell Dalton that I overpowered you and escaped!' by the end of this I am feeling hysterical, my heart is racing, and my voice has gone up a pitch or two.

The only reaction I got was from the minion sat next to me; lets call him Bob. Bob turns to me, laughing in my face, saying 'la puta' before spitting at me. My immediate reaction was to slap him across the face, his reactions are certainly quicker than mine, as he caught my wrist in mid-air whilst backhanding me with his other hand. Ok point taken, shut up Eloise, you are only making this worse for yourself.

TWO

The car slows to a halt outside of a large white washed mansion, it reminded me slightly of the White House in Washington DC. I had never been, but had seen pictures online, and could only assume that they were on the same scale.

All of the minions exited the car, I was unsure if I should stay in the car or attempt to get out also. Before I could make a decision, the car door was opened for me and Dalton was standing there, he had changed clothing since my abduction; no longer in black fatigues, he now wore white, tight fitting chinos, and a white short sleeved shirt opened at the chest, showing a splattering of jet black chest hairs on his muscular chest. The whiteness of his clothing was a direct contrast to his dark tanned skin, a bit like yin and yang.

He reaches across to unclip my seat belt and remove me from the interior of the cool confines of the car, the impact of the heat of the day makes my skin tingle, or could it be that I now find myself in Daltons arms.

Whispering in my ear, his voice full of menace 'Pequena ave, welcome to my home. A few things I need to make you aware of whilst you are here. One; this is my home, treat it with respect. Two; you will not speak to any of the men here. Three; you will make no attempt to leave, and four; I own this whole island, there is no escape!' he looks down at me making sure that this has sunk in, 'understand?' all I can do is nod, succumbing to my fate. 'Good, now let me introduce you to the staff'

I am led up the red, brickwork steps to the vast expanse of the white washed mansion; I am in awe of the sheer size of it! I notice that there is half a dozen women, of varying ages, waiting at the open door; which is flanked either side by two gun-totting minions. Seriously? Why all the madmen wielding weapons, surely if he owns this island it has to be safe, so he shouldn't need all of this weaponry. The women are all standing to attention, most of them looking fearful, awaiting their lord and master, except for one; she is smiling at Dalton and speaking rapidly in a foreign language, she looks pleased to see him, and greets him with a maternal hug. When her eyes rest on my battered face, she takes a sharp intake of breath, she looks at my wrists and the trail of blood leading up the steps behind me. She looks horrified by my appearance, surely I don't look that bad? She slaps him; she actually slaps him! I don't know who she is, but I think I like her.

Dalton responds, sounding apologetic about my appearance, then 'Eloise, this is my housekeeper Magda. She doesn't speak English, not many of my employees do; so do not try to reason with them, my word is law. Magda will show you to your room, and arrange for our site doctor to tend to your injuries. I have an urgent situation that needs taking care of immediately; you will join me for dinner later. Sophia' a young girl no more than 19 steps forward awaiting his orders, which he gives in English, so she must be one of the English speakers here, I need to make friends with her, try to get as much information as to my whereabouts as possible; although he said that there is no escape, I don't quite believe him. 'Take Eloise to her room, draw her a bath. Magda will arrange for Pedro to look at Eloises injuries, you are to stay with her the whole time, I am making you responsible for her; if she breaks any of the rules, then you will be punished alongside her'

Sophia doesn't look happy about this, she opens her mouth as if to argue her position, but one glance at the look on Daltons face, makes her clamp her mouth shut, resigned to carry out his orders.

Magda is talking frantically to someone behind me, I turn to see Blondie approaching me, and fear makes me try to back away from him, remembering the slap I received on the plane, which is still smarting now. This makes him laugh, a full on belly laugh, he seems to revel in the fear I have for him. I am thrown over his shoulder and carried into the cool interior of Daltons home. Followed swiftly by a gushing Magda and a sullen Sophia.

I can't make out much of the interior as I am being carried up a white marble staircase; Blondie is taking two steps at a time and barely breaking a sweat. I can hear Magda speaking behind us, relaying orders into a walkie-talkie, I hear the name Pedro, so assume that she is arranging for him to come and look me over, and treat my injuries. Hopefully he'll bring some really strong painkillers the ones that knock you out, at least then I won't have to suffer Daltons company at dinner. This place feels even bigger on the inside than I first though possible; I can hear the distant noise of people talking and the footsteps of guards on the marble floor. Behind me I can hear the footsteps of Magda and Sophia, quickly joined by a third set and then a male voice speaking in the same tongue.

'Hola, Magda'

'Pedro, el senor quiere que la mires'

'Quien es ella?'

'No lo se, su nombre es Eloise'

Finally I can place the language, Spanish? I think. Why wasn't I more academic at school? Knowing another language, any language, would surely have helped me a little in this situation.

I hear movement at the end of the hallway as a door is opened, I can only assume by a guard. As we approach, I can see two pairs of black military booted feet, so two guards then. Assuming the worst, given Daltons promises of punishing me, I close my eyes, not wanting to see the room I will be kept a prisoner in. My imagination is in overdrive, and I am thinking that I am being taken to a dark medieval cell, with an array of torture devices available. I am shocked to feel sunlight on my eyelids, so I open them cautiously, taking in my surroundings when I am gently placed on a soft surface. This is a normal room, not the dungeon I had been expecting. There is a gloss black queen sized bed, made up with white satin bed linen, with a gloss black bedside table on either side of the bed; it makes the room look like an upmarket boutique hotel. As I look around and take in the monochrome pallet of the interior, I cannot help but wonder if this is a mistake, there are three doors leading off of this room, I assume that one of them must lead to the en-suite facilities, my mind boggles as to where the other two doors might lead. In my head I want to investigate, but somehow I feel as soon as they realise that they have put me in the wrong room, I won't get the opportunity.

Pedro kneels on the white marble floor in front of me, and attempts to take my face in his hands, to look at the marks on my face caused by the slaps from "Blondie" and "Bob". I immediately bat his hands away and move backwards on the black leather sofa. I do not want another person touching me right now; I have simply had enough. Pedro sighs and gently tries again.

'NO!' I scream at him, batting his hands away again. The three people left in the room look taken aback from my sudden outburst, and my refusal of medical treatment. They are even more put out when the two security guards come crashing through the closed door, with their weapons raised, sweeping the room for invaders.

Magda, with a look of concern on her face, shoos the guards out of the room, confirming that there is nothing to worry about.

'Miss, Pedro need to check your wounds. He the Island Doctor, he not hurt you' Sophia, speaking in broken English is kneeling in front of me now, with a pleading look on her face. 'Please, you let him look. We have much trouble if you not'

Really? Is that supposed to make me roll over and beg? They have chosen to work for a Neanderthal, why should it bother me if they find themselves in trouble? Although, if I do find an opportunity to escape; I am not going to get very far with the state that I am currently in at the moment.

'Ok, he can look at my foot, and remove any glass that is left in there. If he leaves me some painkillers and ointment for my wrists I will do the rest' I am hoping that the tone of my voice is given with enough conviction to make them realise that this is not open for a debate, a discussion or a compromise.

Luckily my words have some weight, because after much to-ing and fro-ing in their native tongue, Pedro shrugs his shoulders and carefully starts to inspect my foot. He gives me an injection around the injury, which I am told will numb it enough to remove the glass, I am so thankful for this as I have no doubt that it would have hurt like hell.

After removing the glass and sealing the wound with stitches, Pedro leaves, giving instructions to Magda and Sophia on how to bandage my foot after my bath. In my head, I know that there is no way anyone is coming anywhere near me right now. I can bandage it myself; I can also rub the ointment on to my wrists and take care of my battered face. I've been doing things for myself for a long time now, I have become self-sufficient; not through choice, but through necessity, so I know that I do not need anybody's help

Whilst Pedro, Magda and Sophia are deep in conversation, I take the opportunity to hobble to the large glass doors that are adjacent to the bed. The view is simply breath taking, nothing but crystal clear ocean for miles, my heart sinks, the only way to escape this island is either by plane or by boat. I look down at the road that I assume we travelled on from the airstrip, following it's path I notice a cove, with, what looks like a mooring and a couple of speedboats. I wonder if there is a way to climb down from here, the cove doesn't look that far, if I am left alone for long enough, I am almost certain that I could make it. I try the handle of the doors, thinking that they will more than likely locked; to my surprise they open with such force as a strong gust takes them out of my hands, taking me unaware. I try to steady myself, forgetting my injured foot, and cry out in pain as it makes contact with the cold floor.

Magda and Sophia are next to me within seconds, checking if I am ok. I reassure them that I am fine and wave them away. If I am absolutely honest, I am anything but fine. I am so confused; I have been forcibly taken from my home, and as far as the world is concerned I died in a fire, and yet I am being treated like a guest by the staff of the person who caused all of this.

Once Magda is satisfied that I haven't injured myself further, she leaves the room through one of the three doors I spotted earlier, clucking and speaking in a chastising tone the whole time, eventually the sound of her voice is drowned out by the sound of bath water running.

'Come, I show you' Sophia opens the second door to show me a vast dressing room, it is actually larger than my bedroom at home, 'Senor has clothes sent for you. Look, they nice, they ok?' she is touching the clothes hanging from hangers around the room; it looks more like the clothing section in a department store, than a wardrobe. I have never seen so many pairs of shoes, dresses, blouses or trousers. I covertly look at the shoes, hoping against hope, for a nice pair of trainers to make my planned escape easier, unfortunately they are all heels; even the 1' ones look impossible to run fast in, I feel deflated.

Magda calls from the bathroom, telling Sophia that the bath is ready for me. At last I'll get some privacy. I enter the bathroom as Magda leaves, and swiftly shut and bolt the door.

'Miss?' Sophia is hammering at the door; does she really think I need an audience? 'You let me in now? Senor, he say, I stay with you. Please'

'I'm a grown arse women; I do not need, nor want your help, or an audience. Go and bother someone else,' I shout with my back against the closed door. I can't help feeling slightly mean, after all she is just doing her job, I almost buckle and let her in, as I hear her voice pleading for entry again, then I remember how and why I am here, and who her employer is. Tough titties, Sophia, go harp to someone who actually cares.

Eventually, the sound of Sophias whining and hammering dissipate, so I move away from the door and look around the bathroom. Again the same colour palette of black and white, with chrome bath furniture. It looks very sleek, the bath is sunken into the floor, and is large enough to accommodate at least three people comfortably. There is a separate walk in shower for two people at the far end of the room, there doesn't appear to be a shower screen, so I can only assume that you would call this a wet room. The black tiles extend from floor to ceiling with all of the sanitary wear in white marble. One wall has a floor to ceiling mirror, and my breath catches when I see my reflection; my hair looks as if I have been dragged through a hedge backwards again, and my face is grey; reminding me of a cartoon character when the blood drains from it, there is dried blood from the corner of my mouth down to my chin; courtesy of "Blondie", my mouth is swollen from where he hit me, and I can see a bruise already beginning to form. My eye is so swollen, that I am surprised that I can see out of it, I swear that I can make out a red handprint from "Bobs" slap, that is going to leave one hell of a bruise. But what troubles me the most, is the eyes staring back at me; they don't look like my eyes, they have lost their spark, they are devoid of emotion; and have become black holes.

Unable to look at my reflection any longer, and force myself to succumb to the realisation that it is indeed my reflection looking back at me, I take some of the painkillers left by Pedro, before stripping off and stepping into the bath.

The water temperature is perfect, and I feel my skin start to pinch with the heat. The smell from the suds is soothing my weary mind, with the water having the same effect on my aching body. I tip my head back and submerge myself in the water, just leaving my face above the water line, and close my eyes. I can no longer see anything, or hear anything; I can pretend to myself that I am safe, at home, in my own bath. I start to relax and begin humming to myself, no song in particular, just a gentle hum, similar to what a mother might hum to soothe her distressed child.

Sensing movement in the room, I open my eyes and am startled to see Dalton standing over me, looking down and smiling. It takes me a moment to remind myself of my surroundings, I must have drifted off as the water temperature has certainly cooled a few degrees, and my fingers look like prunes.

'What are you doing in here? How did you get in? I locked the door'

'Relax pequena ave, this is a Jack and Jill bathroom' sensing my confusion, 'I came through the door that leads to my room, we share this bathroom, you only locked the one door, not both' he explains.

Another door? He's lying. I peer in the direction that he pointed, and sure enough there is another door; how could I have missed that? I blame my addled state of mind.

'Sophia was concerned that something had happened to you, so she came looking for me, and I'm glad that she did. Or I may have missed your little show'

Little show? What on earth is he talking about? Looking down I realise that the suds have all but gone leaving me completely exposed, my erect pink nipples protruding the waterline. Instinct makes me use my hands to reclaim my dignity; I can feel the tell-tale heat of embarrassment rising in my face. Trying my hardest not to make eye contact with Dalton, but when he moves closer, I cannot help but look up at him. I take in the beauty of his features for the first time; his perfectly chiselled square jaw, along with high cheekbones that women would die to have. With his dark olive skin and black hair, swept to one side, he is one very attractive man. His white shirt does nothing to hide the perfectly toned body lurking beneath it. Trying my hardest to ignore the raw animal magnetism that is trying to draw me in. In another lifetime, I could certainly see myself going out of my way for him to notice me; but now, I just want to shrivel up and die.

'Pequena ave, you delight me in ways that should infuriate me. I have already seen you naked, so why do you feel the need to cover up in front of me?' without breaking eye contact, he raises one eyebrow, with a grin that doesn't quite reach his eyes, 'I will have to ask Sophia to remove the clothes from your wardrobe, and make you walk around naked, my men will certainly enjoy looking at your body,' he laughs at the shocked look on my face, 'unless of course, you remove your hands immediately.'

Weighing up my options, I slowly remove my hands, feeling the shame wash over me as I look down yet again.

'Ah, mi pequeno pajaro, much better, and a very wise decision'

He slowly walks towards me, like a lion stalking its prey, and all I can do is lay there motionless, hoping that the lion does not pounce on me, hoping beyond hope that he will leave. No such luck. He sits on the marble floor next to the bath, looking down at me, and before I have time to react, he snakes his arm underneath my back supporting my weight, and making it impossible for me to move away from him. With his free hand he gently touches the injuries on my face, I wasn't expecting him to be so gentle, and wait with baited breath for the slap that I was sure to come. 'I am sorry that they hurt you, I will make them pay' he brushes some unruly hair gently off of my face, cupping my chin forcing me to look into his eyes, he looks sad; sad and angry, 'even with the bruises, you are so beautiful, my little bird'

He takes my mouth in a crushing kiss, trying to force his tongue into my mouth, I clamping my jaw shut with all of my might, in a desperate bid to refuse him entry. His hand travels down my neck, traces the sensitive part of my collarbone, leading to the valley between my breasts.

His touch is so sensual, almost as if he is trying to commit my form to memory. He moves his hand to take possession of my breast, and begins to gently knead it; using the pad of his forefinger and the nail of his thumb he gently squeezes my erect nipple, the mixture of pleasure and pain shooting through my body, forces me to take a sharp intake of breath, leaving my mouth wide open for the coming onslaught of his tongue. He's thumb and forefinger are now alternating between gentle kneading and harsh pinching, causing an assault on my senses, it feels so good that I begin to kiss Dalton back with almost as much passion and ferocity as him.

Moving my arms behind his head to deepen the kiss. His hand starts to trace circles around the mound of each of my breasts before beginning to head further south. The feeling mounting inside of me is making me forget myself, I cannot remember having this feeling with anyone else before. His hand continues to trace small circles on the flat of my stomach, whilst heading to the cluster of nerves between my thighs, thinking he is going to touch me there I hold my breath in anticipation; not entirely sure if this is what I want to happen. As if sensing my apprehension, he stops all contact and stands, quickly striding away from me.

Suddenly I am cold, confused and embarrassed by my reaction towards him. I have heard of reports that victims in similar circumstances suffer with Stockholm syndrome, but surely it is too soon for this to rear it's ugly head? I mean I hate him, but I can't help being attracted to him at the same time.

'Mi pequeno pajaro, I will not rape you, you have my word. When I take you, and I will take you, you will beg for me to do so' he left a slight pause to allow this to sink in. 'now get dressed and join me for dinner, you must be hungry and Magda is an amazing chef. She makes the best Quesadillas this side of Mexico'

With one last look at me, he turns on his heel and leaves me to my thoughts. For a second there I thought he was going to continue where he left off. I am not sure if I am yet strong enough for another of his onslaughts. I need to find a way to man up and find a way out of this situation, with my virginity still intact.

Worrying about the repercussions if I disobey him again, I dutifully exit the bath to dry myself and find something to wear for dinner. Although he gave his word that he wouldn't rape me, that doesn't mean that he would stop his men from doing so. What was it he said? Oh yes, "this side of Mexico", does this mean we are near Mexico? If we are, then I am a long way from home. Without a passport, any form of transportation and no money, my chances of escape are becoming smaller by the hour.

After thoroughly drying myself, and towel drying my hair, I find Sophia pacing in front of the bathroom door; nibbling anxiously on her nails. Hearing the click of the bathroom door, she stopped pacing to look at me. The conflict of emotions on her face were easy to read; as if she was deciding whether to be angry at being locked out, or relieved that I was still alive, and hadn't done anything stupid. Eventually she decided on relief, rushing at me whilst gushing in Spanish. Holding my hand she led me into the dressing room, pulling dresses out from their hangers for me to look at.

'This one; so pretty; match eyes,' the dress she was pulling out was indeed beautiful; a brilliant blue, tea length, chiffon gown. It looked as if it would hug my curves in all of the right places; the only draw back was the fact that despite it being a halter-neck, it would drop to my navel; showing far too much cleavage for my liking.

According to Sophia, all of them were pretty and would match my eyes. Yes the dresses were all gorgeous, but they were either too short, too low cut or both. Feeling no desire to dress like a hooker, I rummage through the draws, finally selecting a pair of skin tight, low slung black jeans, matched with a black figure hugging vest top. I also managed to find a pair of black pants with a matching bra, which is the perfect size for my ample assets. Holding the door open for Sophia, indicating that I do not need company whilst dressing. I removed the now damp towel from my body, but keep the one wrapped around my hair in place, and quickly dressed, aware that someone could come in at any moment, and I really didn't want a repeat performance of the bathtub incident.

Once dressed, I continued to rummage the banks of

drawers trying to find a hairbrush to tease the copious amount of knots that had once again formed in my waist length black hair.

Sophia hearing the drawers being opened and closed, tentatively knocks on the door, whilst poking her head around the frame, 'Miss? I help you, yes'

As if comprehending what I was searching for, she opens a drawer and pulled out a wide toothed comb. Reached for the comb, I try to make it clear, without being rude, that I can comb my own hair.

The look on Sophias face, when she took in the outfit I was wearing, was clear; she did not approve.

'Miss, you change, Senor not like this'

'Really? What a shame. To be perfectly honest with you I don't really care what Senor likes' without realising, this was said with more venom than was intended, I feel the need to immediately apologise when I see the hurt on Sophias face. 'Sophia, I'm sorry, I shouldn't have said that.'

'Is ok, miss'

Feeling the need to make things right with her, I sit at the dressing table stool and allow her to brush my long locks; after all, if she were to be my companion, it wouldn't do to fall out with her. She may, hopefully, be able to help me escape.

Suddenly a thought struck me, I had to know what Dalton had been calling me; it was said so softly, like a term of endearment. I also wanted to know what "Bob" had called me just before hitting me; I'm no rocket scientist, but I am sure as hell that it wasn't a term of endearment.

'Sophia? Can I ask you something?'

'Yes, Miss' Sophia didn't even look up from her task of combing my hair; as if this situation was a regular occurrence for her, which made me even more curious.

Has this happened before? When? Who with? Did they escape? How did they get away? I need to stop thinking like a journalist and try to concentrate on my current situation. Why do I always need to get the scoop? This is what got me here in the first place.

'Sophia, what does "mi pequeno pajaro" mean?' I look into the mirror, trying to make eye contact with her.

'It mean "Little Bird" miss. Senor say this to you, I hear him. He like you' a sly smile reached the corner of her lips, but it didn't quite make it to her eyes; I can't help feeling that she looks slightly jealous.

'And, what does "La Puta" mean?

Sophias sharp intake of breathe, and the dropping of her jaw, told me everything that I needed to know; definitely not a term of endearment. 'Miss, it is not nice, I cannot say'

'Ok, I understand, I'll ask Dalton'

'Miss, no, he be angry. Who say this?'

'One of the men, just before he gave me this,' for emphasis I point at the handprint on my face. Sophia looks shocked; I am not entirely sure where, or how, she thought my injuries had occurred. My initial estimation put Sophias age at around 19 years old, but now, due to her naivety, I find myself recalculating this, and putting her much younger; possibly even 15, what on earth makes a young girl find employment in a place like this, with men like these? She seems so sweet and innocent; I can't help feeling maternal and a sense of wanting to protect her from the men on this Island, especially Bob and Blondie.

'Miss, I tell you, but not say to Senor, make him angry, ok?' she waited until I nodded in agreement, before telling me, 'miss, it mean "bitch or whore",'

Wow, I am speechless; bitch I can understand, sort of, but whore? I'm a virgin for crying out loud. I can feel the anger rising inside of me, and my blood is boiling, I need to calm myself down before I do something that I will later regret. Admittedly, judging by the amount of personnel I have already witnessed on the Island, the chances of bumping into "Bob" are pretty slim, but in my current state of mind, I cannot guarantee that I wouldn't give him a piece of my mind. Plus now that I know he is the "hit first, ask questions later" kind of person, I will be more prepared on our next encounter.

When Sophia is satisfied that she has managed to sufficiently tame my unruly locks, she sets about blow-drying it back into it's poker straight style. It's actually quite relaxing having someone do this for you, a bit like an Indian head massage, but without the spiky thing that is sometimes used.

As if on cue, as soon as Sophia has finished, there is a gentle tap at the door. Turning, I see Dalton standing there in a white three-piece tuxedo. Suddenly I feel underdressed and embarrassed, realising why Sophia was so keen for me to wear one of the many dresses available. If Dalton was displeased with my choice of clothing, he hid it very well. Sophia, however, looking worried, shifted her gaze to the floor and shuffled quickly out of the room.

Following Sophias rushed exit from the room, I find my gaze meeting Daltons; blanching at the look of pure lust in his eyes. Feeling a tightening in my core; the sensitive area between my legs begins to pulsate the with anticipation of what is to come. If he could devour me on the spot, I am in no doubt that he would.

With one gazelle-like stride he is on me. Before I have time to react, or compose myself, I find that I am held captive in his crushing arms, his lips finding mine with a passionate frenzy. I must have left my brain at home, because I am kissing him back with the same force and urgency. All of a sudden he clasps my legs, spreads them to each side of his waist and carries me to the bed; without removing the contact of his lips on mine, he gently places me on the soft mattress, with him on top me.

I can feel his rock-hard member between us as he gyrates his hips; catching the sensitive cluster of nerves at the top of my thighs, it feels so good and causes my nerves to throb. His hands lift at the hem of my top, seeking out my breasts and gently kneading them through my bra, teasing my now erect nipples. With a swift movement he rips my bra from its purchase on my breasts; exposing my bare flesh to his wanton hands. Feeling wetness in my pants that I haven't felt before as the throbbing sensation makes me gyrate my hips to meet with his. Moving my hands behind his head, and taking clumps of his hair in them, forcing the kiss to be deepened as his tongue ravishes my mouth. Hearing him groan into my mouth, makes me quicken my gyrating hips, eager for more. My breasts suddenly feel cold as he reaches behind his head and clasps my hands in his; moving them above my head holding them both in place with one of his. Then his assault of my now exposed breasts continue, I feel powerless; overcome with the sensation of how good this feels, and how turned on I am. He dips his head down and begins sucking on one of my erect nipples, while teasing and pinching the other with his thumb and forefinger; my breath catches on a long moan. He alternates sucking, with blowing cold air on my extremely sensitive nipple, chuckling to himself at the reaction this is causing in me.

 His free hand begins to trail down to the fly on my jeans, and deftly opens them, seeking the warm wetness buried inside. He rubs my sensitive mound with his fingers, quickening his touch, revelling in the sensations he is stirring deep inside of me. I can feel the mounting pressure of an orgasm screaming to be released, I hear myself screaming his name as the orgasm takes over; racking my body, after wave, upon wave takes hold. His searching hands do not relent in their assault on my senses; teasing yet more explosions from my exhausted body.

 I moan in disappointment as his hand moves away from my throbbing mound, eager for him to place it back there and ravish it once more. With one hand he removes my jeans and pants, then continues to tease my clitoris, causing shock waves to ripple through me. Moving his fingers between my lips, he makes his way to the wet, warm opening of my vagina; revelling in the feel of how wet I am for him. Teasing the folds of my labia, I moan in ecstasy. Yearning for a deeper contact, I thrust my hips into his waiting hand. He moves his position so that he is now kneeling on the floor between my legs, I gasp as his tongue makes contact with my clitoris; I can feel another orgasm coming and with a slow sucking motion, I explode on the tide of another powerful orgasm. My body is trembling in ecstasy, but I still want more. I want it all. I want him in me. Fucking me like a Demon!

 'Mi pequeno pajaro, I can't wait to punish you' I hear him say as he unzips his fly, and I freeze; suddenly coming to my senses and remembering where I am, and who this is.

 As if sensing the change in my demeanour and my willingness to partake in his seduction, he stops and looks up me.

The look of wanton lust is quickly fading away my face, and shame sets in as I look down at my exposed body, still trembling from the last explosion of orgasms.

'Stop, I can't,' I stutter, trembling, fearful that he is at the point of no return and will take what he wants anyway. Seeing the thunderous look on his face, I explain 'I'm a virgin'

'You're fucking with me! How can you get to be 23 year of age and have never been screwed by someone?' he stands in frustration, causing his trousers to fall to his knees. I can't help but stifle a chuckle at him stood there in his white tuxedo, looking immaculate from the waist up, his rock hard member protruding beneath his shirt, with his trousers around his knees. I stare at it; it's impossible not to, it is not only long, but it is wide as well, it looks about the same size as my forearm.

As if sensing where my gaze is focused he chuckles and moves to lie on top of me again. He starts stroking my cleft again, trying to work me up into a passionate frenzy, and take me to the point of no return. I am ashamed of how eager my body is and how quickly it can betray me. As I have an internal struggle of mind over matter, I feel his manhood trying to gain entry to soft flesh, prodding gently, seeking access. I start to tremble, but this time it is fear that is making me tremble, all thoughts of orgasms, and the ecstasy that he can provide are gone, I am now a startled rabbit fighting for survival.

'Please' I cry, tears streaming down my face. 'You gave me your word; you said you wouldn't rape me. I do not want this, or you' I add for good measure.

This makes him stop just as his member was about to delve deep inside of me, if I were to make any sudden movement, my hymen would be broken and I would be undone, begging to be fucked harder. It took all of my strength to lie as still as possible, waiting for him to fight his inner demons; one wanting to take possession of me, and the other wanting to do the right thing.

I wait frozen with fear, not entirely sure which one I wanted to win the battle.

With a deep sigh he moves his position, so each of his hands are either side of my head, looking down into my eyes, trying to gauge my emotions. 'You're sure you don't want this' giving a little wiggle of his hips, I can feel his member move side to side at the point of entry, yet it doesn't try to gain deeper access to my warm, wet tunnel.

'Yes' I reply breathlessly.

With a grunt he moves away from me, putting a good ten spaces between us. 'I suggest you cover yourself up; I am fighting with all of my will power not to take what you so evidently want to give me. Go and get yourself dressed'

I jump off of the bed and run to the dressing room, eager to be away from him, fearful that he will follow through on what he has started, a small part of me really wants him to; to take what my body so desperately wants to give him, but self-preservation wins out every time. I lock the dressing room door behind me, and begin frantically opening and closing draws trying to find something to wear that isn't figure hugging, too short or too low cut. Deflated I discover that there isn't anything; so I decide on another pair of jeans and t-shirt.

When I return to the bedroom I discover that Dalton hasn't moved, it is as if he is frozen in time, rooted to the spot. The look on his face has changed though, the look of lust is still there, but now a look of anger has also set in. I can't help but feel confused.

'Come here,' he orders with a voice I don't recognise.

I stand mouth agape, rooted to the spot, unable to move.

'The way I see it, you have two choices. You come here as ordered, or I come over there and take what I want'

The look on his face leaves me in no doubt that he will follow through on his threat this time, so I slowly cross the room to stand in front of him, careful to leave enough space between us so that I don't feel his member against my stomach.

Looking down at me, 'get on your knees' he commands, all of the warmth has left his face, and his voice. 'Let me remind you, I don't like asking twice. Get on your knees now!'

With little option I crouch on my knees wondering where on earth this was going.

'Open your mouth'

I am shocked at what he is suggesting, but if it's a choice between this or the other, I choose this.

'Wider' before I know it, he forces his penis into my open mouth. Slowly thrusting until my mouth grows accustomed to his girth, he quickens his pace, occasionally thrusting deeper, hitting the back of my throat, causing me to gag. He grabs clumps of my hair in both of his hands, forcing my head forward with each of his thrusts, causing me to gag repeatedly and cutting off my air supply. Tears are streaming down my face; from the repeated gagging, being starved of oxygen, and the sheer shame of my situation, and of what is being forced upon me. His pace quickens even more, so much so that I cannot tell the difference between each thrusting stroke. I feel him start to swell as he becomes ready to climax. With a guttural sound I feel his hot semen being pumped into my mouth, hitting the back of my throat, leaving me no option but to swallow. He stands there, not releasing his purchase of my hair, waiting for his orgasm to dissipate. Slowly his hands drop to his sides, and he steps back from me, his now flaccid member falling from my mouth and slapping against his thigh.

Without a word, or even looking at me on my knees, he pulls his trousers up, tucks in his shirt, and straightens his tie, leaving the room without even looking at me on my knees.

I feel violated. Yes, admittedly, he kept his word and didn't rape me, but what just happened certainly feels like rape. I curl into a ball on the floor and sob my heart out, eventually crying myself to sleep.

THREE

This is where Sophia finds me sometime later, still curled up in the foetal position, on the hard marble floor. She gently nudges me to wake me from my slumber, 'Miss'

Feeling like an obstinate child I refuse to open my eyes, I do not want to wake up, and I certainly do not want to face my new reality. Even though my body is aching from lying on the cold floor for god knows how long, I just want to stay here, frozen in time.

Sophia continues in her persistent coaxing, which eventually has its desired effect. As I open my eyes to look up at her, and take in the dim light of early dusk, she looks relieved and a little confused. 'Miss, why floor? Bed?' to which she points; the large bed seemingly calling my name.

It would be so nice to envelop myself in the soft folds of the covers, but all I can think about is how my treacherous body betrayed itself on that very bed not so long ago. Refusing to go there again, I push it aside and raise myself from the floor, smoothing my hair from my face. A few stray strands catch on my split lip, and I realise that Daltons actions have made the wound reopen and begin to bleed again.

I walk to the bathroom to assess the damage that has been done, barely recognising the woman staring back at me; dried blood making a trail from her lip to her chin with a ghostly pale complexion; the colour of the blood a stark contrast to the whiteness of my skin, but what shocked me the most was the haunted look in the eyes that stared back at me; eyes swollen and red from the recent crying, my pupils appearing to consume the piercing blue of my irises. I need to pull myself together; and find my inner strength, to find the power within to fight back. If they mean to kill me, then at least I'll go out fighting.

Forming a plan of action, I splash cold water over my face, taking care not to open the cut on my lip again. Finding a clean facecloth I soak it in cold water, squeezing the excess out and press it onto eyes that are red and swollen from crying. I will not let him see me like this; I will not let him know the effect that he has on me. I will never allow him to touch me again, I vow to myself silently. Although, truth be told, despite feeling resolute in my outlook towards him, a little niggle tells me that if he approaches me with warmth and tenderness; I will more than likely cave.

As I leave the bathroom, my skin prickles and the fine hairs on my arms stand to attention, there can be only one thing that would have this affect on me; without even looking around I know that Dalton is in my room again; his hungry eyes following my every move. Without looking in his direction, I enter the dressing room and lock the door firmly closed behind me. I am tempted to move the dressing table stool in front of the door, for good measure, but fear that they will hear the scraping of the heavy object across the carpeted floor; after all, I do not wish to appear childish. Plus I do not want him to know the effect his presence is already having on me. Feeling his close proximity, even in the short space of time that it took to walk from the bathroom to the dressing room, has such an immediate effect on me, something that I hadn't bargained for; my heart is pounding in chest and my hands are cold and clammy to the touch, I can already feel the tell tale throb of excitement and a wetness between my legs; a mixture of fear and sexual anticipation.

'Miss' Sophia is knocking gently on the door, persistent as ever. 'Senor say you have dinner now'

'Tell him to piss off, I'm not hungry' I am so sick of him telling me what to do; get dressed; come here; get on your knees. The memories of what happened come flooding back to my mind and I begin to urge, trying my hardest to dispel the thoughts, keep quiet and not be sick.

'Miss, you ok?'

Such a simple question, am I ok? If I am honest with myself, I am anything but ok. Standing in the dressing room, trying to decide whether or not to reply, I hear a thud and then an almighty crash, as the dressing room door comes to rest on the floor a few metres away from my feet, looking at the opening where the door was once situated, I see Dalton standing in the broken frame. The noise that was created from Dalton kicking the door off of its hinges makes me jump back, startled, and looking like a frightened rabbit in his direction. Misreading the situation, he begins to approach me, reaching with both hands ready to cup my face.

'Stop, don't come near me' to give weight to my voice I put both hands up and move back from him.

He continues to move towards me, whilst I continue to move away from him. Desperate to maintain the space between us until my back hits the wall, and I have nowhere left to run.

'I'm warning you, come one step closer, or touch me again, and you will be sorry' I add as much venom to my voice as possible, it sounded so alien to me that I was shocked at the way it sounded as it left my lips.

Dalton pauses for a second and then begins to roar with laughter. Tears are streaming down his face whilst he continues to laugh uncontrollably. Then as if a switch has been turned off, he stops just as quickly as he started. Before I know it, he is standing in front of me; so close that my chest was grazing his toned abdomen with each breath I take. I look up at him in shock at how quickly his emotions can change; he is like Jekyll and Hide. His close proximity causes my nipples to bud, and my mound to throb painfully; I feel so wet and turned on. The smell of his cologne is putting my senses into over drive; I have always had a problem with the effect some scents have on me; I have been known to approach complete strangers to ask what cologne or perfume they are wearing.

'Sophia, leave us' he barks, barely removing his eyes from mine. Waiting for the click of the outer bedroom door, indicating that it had been closed, before continuing 'Remember this' clasping my head in his hands, he moves his face down to whisper vehemently, 'you are mine, if I choose to fuck that pretty mouth of yours again, then I will' looking deep into my eyes, our noses touching, making sure that what he has said has sunk in, his gaze trails to my mouth, 'such a pretty little mouth' he kisses me tenderly to begin with, gradually deepening the kiss, nibbling and sucking on my lips, the sensation sending shock waves through my core. He breaks contact with my mouth, causing me to moan in complaint. Looking down at my now visibly erect nipples, before once again looking into my eyes 'I hear the words coming out of your mouth but they mean nothing, your body tells me everything that I need to know,' he reaches for my breasts;

cupping them gently, gradually increasing the force with which he begins to knead them, squeezing my nipples, he watches as my breath comes in ragged gasps, my mouth slightly open, with the expectation of what is to come. 'Your body yearns to feel me inside of you, fucking you deep. When will you admit to yourself that it is what you want?' His mouth comes down into a crashing kiss, his tongue darting into my mouth; his hands wandering further south, seeking the sweet spot between my thighs.

'Senor?' the sound of Sophias voice makes him pause.

Looking into my eyes, I can see the lust for me burning there. I watch with fascination as the lust is quickly replaced with irritation at Sophias interruption. Without breaking eye contact with me he turns his head towards his shoulder, shouting angrily in Sophias general direction 'I told you to leave us'.

What followed was a conversation spoken entirely in Spanish. Dalton appearing angry at being interrupted, whilst chastising an apologetic Sophia. Whereas I couldn't be any happier, thank god she came back when she did, Christ knows how far it would have gone this time. With each new assault, I can feel my resolve weakening even further. I can't help but grin to myself, thinking; "Saved by the Sophia."

Once Sophia had left again, Dalton turns with a blank expression on his face, 'It appears that you have been saved from me yet again. Sophia has just informed me, that Magda is cross that the dinner she has prepared for us is spoiling.' Misreading the grin on my face he adds 'but don't worry, we will pick up where we left off later. I have plans for you.'

With a slight bow he offers his arm to me, 'shall we go to dinner?' I find the change in his demeanour disconcerting; he shifts his emotions so quickly my brain is struggling to keep up.

Without taking his arm, I push past him, which causes him to laugh in delight yet again.　Stopping in the hallway, suddenly realising that I have no clue which direction I should head in. Although, rather childishly, I stated that I wasn't hungry; I am, in actual fact, famished. The smell of food cooking in the kitchen is making my mouth water, and my stomach begins to growl in complaint. I cannot wait to try some of Magdas cooking, it has been a long time since I had a proper home cooked meal; I was always too busy working long hours, so finding time to cook was nigh on impossible, so I tended to rely on ready meals; which invariably tasted like cardboard or were so bland they were tasteless.

I can feel Dalton standing behind me as my senses begin to prickle; placing his hand around my waist; he guides me towards the staircase I was unceremoniously carried up earlier. Steering me out of the earshot of the two guards stationed outside of my bedroom door, he whispers in my ear, 'you really are a delight, I am so looking forward to teaching you some manners'

Seeing the look on his face, I have suddenly lost my appetite. How on earth I am going to find the strength to come out of this unscathed. I can already feel myself changing inside; he is correct I yearn for his touch, and I yearn to feel his girth ravaging me and taking me to places I have never been before.

The dining room that we enter is as large as you would expect of a house of this size.　Again decorated in the same monochrome pallet of black and white, with little touches of red creeping in from the candles and the dinner service, which was laid out on the table. The black gloss granite table, is being held in place by a solitary central leg; considering the table was large enough to seat ten people comfortably, the balancing act needed to keep it there must have been quite a challenge. The chairs are upholstered in a white leather with black gloss legs. With the black marble flooring, and the bottom half of the walls also being black; the optical illusion that is created, makes the chairs look as if they are suspended in mid-air. One wall was constructed of sheets of glass, which were open and concertinaed against one another; the occasional breeze causing the white muslin drapes to billow in the wind; carrying with it the scent of the ocean and a delicate floral perfume.

My stomach grumbles noisily, as the smells emanating from the buffet placed in the centre of the table hits my nose, beside me, Dalton, with his hand still in the small of my back, chuckles at the noise.

"Hungry Mi pequeno pajaro?' looking down at me with a boyish grin on his face, he truly is magnificent to look at. Guiding me towards one of the heavy chairs, he pulls it away from the table, and waits for me to be seated, before taking the seat next to me. 'Magda didn't know what you liked, so she has cooked everything,' pointing to each of the dishes, he made sure that I was aware of the heat, the name and rough ingredients of each of them.

I was captivated by how charming he was able to become, I couldn't help but take quick glances at his face to check that this was the same person who had treated me so badly earlier.

Sensing that I was out of my comfort zone, and not entirely happy with helping myself to any of the food on display, Dalton picked up the plate in front of me, and started adding a small selection of food from each of the plates that he had described as mild. Once he was happy that I did indeed have a mountain of food piled high on the plate in front of me, he began filling his own plate with everything he termed as 'extra, extra spicy'. Making sure that we both had a full glass of a fruity red wine, he began to eat; not taking his eyes off of me; making a mental note of the reaction each of the foods had on me.

Cautiously, I began picking at the food on my plate; uncomfortably aware that every mouthful I took was being watched. Unaccustomed to having an audience; albeit an audience of one, whilst eating, I appeared to be pushing more food around the plate than what has actually entered my mouth. Feeling embarrassment at my behaviour, I pushed my knife and fork together to indicate that I have finished, with a polite 'that was lovely, thank you.'

Whatever emotion Dalton was feeling, his face didn't disclose it. 'Mi pequeno pajaro, you have barely eaten a thing. Do you not like the food? Perhaps it is too hot for you. I will ask Magda to prepare something else for you'

'No, please, I'm fine. Honestly, the food was lovely. You were right, Magda is an excellent chef.'

'She will be pleased to hear that you liked her food, although she will be concerned that you could not possibly make that judgement, based alone on the small amount that you have eaten. Please eat some more, you are a guest in my home, it would not do for you to leave the table hungry. Otherwise Magda will be cross with me and may just hit me again.' Pouting his lips and creasing his forehead into a worried frown, he reminded me of a little boy that was about to get chastised, and I couldn't help but laugh at him.

Relenting, I said 'ok, I'll eat some more, I wouldn't want Magda to punish you' then all of a sudden my thoughts went to his promise of punishing me, and I couldn't help but feel slightly excited; it had to be the wine that was having this effect on me, I could think of no other reason for it. Deciding that perhaps I should cut back on the amount of alcohol I was consuming, I pushed my glass away.

'Do you not like the wine? I have others, I'll have another bottle opened for you to try' clicking his fingers, a waiter that I hadn't spotted earlier was by his side within seconds. After Dalton had put in a request for another bottle to be opened, the waiter clicked his heels; astounded, as I couldn't believe that he actually clicked his heels as he left to do carry out Daltons orders.

'Please don't go to any trouble. I am not a big drinker, so one glass is usually my limit' I try to explain, hoping that he'll call the waiter back, and cancel his request.

As if assessing my limitations, he looks deep into my eyes, appearing to become lost in thought, the clicking of the waiters footsteps on hard marble behind him, snaps him out of his reverie. A boyish grin plays at the corners of his mouth as if he has made a decision.

'You must try this wine' seeing my reticence as the wine from earlier is already having an affect on me, he adds 'it is from my private vineyard and it retails for $500, it would be a shame for it to go to waste. Please just one glass'

The wine already in my system has me agreeing to his request. I must admit, although I am by no means a connoisseur, the wine was delicious. Sweet and fruity; like a fruity syrup, but not at all sickly. Before I knew it my glass was empty and Dalton was topping it up. I notice that he isn't drinking this wine, preferring the already opened bottle from earlier. Food forgotten, the wine was going straight to my head, and I was beginning to feel slightly tipsy.

'Mi pequeno pajaro, are you ok?'

'Hmm? Yes, yes I'm fine' my addled brain was struggling to keep up with him, 'did you say something?'

'I was asking what made you decide to become a journalist'

'Oh, why?'

'I'm just curious' shifting in his seat he turns to look at me; placing his arm across the back of my chair, his fingers begin to trace along the back of my neck and the length of my collarbone. My nerve endings are on fire, each fresh touch causing ripples of desire. 'I expected to find a middle aged hag when I discovered a journalist was investigating one of my interests, not someone as young and delectable as you'

A soft moan escapes my partially opened mouth, the ability to speak has left me; I am unable to think of a reply, as his touch has made my brain turn to jelly. All I can think is how amazing his touch feels, I lean into his hand, trying to prolong the contact.

'Come little one, you appear to have had too much wine, let's walk in the gardens and get some fresh air'

Helping me to my feet, he places his arm firmly around my waist; taking possession of my small frame. Stepping through the large doors, I find myself in a tropical paradise; a large grassy area, surrounded by borders containing large shrubs in varying shades of green, interspersed with the most gorgeous coloured flowers I have ever seen. The smell of the ocean, the freshly cut grass and the flora was intoxicating. The fresh air coupled with the wine I had consumed made me feel unstable and dizzy.

Worried that I may fall on the uneven flagstones, I place my hand on Daltons abdomen. My involuntary movement causing him to come to an abrupt standstill, whilst I continue in my forward motion and almost fall onto the floor; with his cat like reflexes I quickly find myself in his arms, being crushed against his chest, his lips showering my face with longing kisses, before consuming my mouth in an ever deepening kiss.

My mouth yielded quickly to his invading tongue, my tongue quickly matching the rhythm of his. Feeling every ripple of his muscular torso beneath my touch, my hands are in overdrive, desperate to seek out every groove on his abdomen. I moan softly as his hands find the perfect curve of my arse, pulling me closer so I can feel his arousal. I want him inside me so badly, I reach behind him, grabbing his firm, perfectly formed backside and pull him even closer. This action takes him by complete surprise, his breath catches in his throat and I swear that I can feel his rock hard cock pulsating against me. I moan in delight at the reaction he has towards me, in this small moment in time I am feeling empowered and in control.

'I want you so badly it hurts, Mi pequeno pajaro' he whispers breathlessly in my ear, grinding his pelvis against me; sending shock waves through me at each new touch of his arousal, 'say you want me too, and I'll make you mine forever'

Knowing full well, that whatever I choose to decide to do in this very moment, I will probably live to regret forever, I look deep into his eyes, whispering 'I want you too, make me yours'

His lips come crashing to meet mine as a guttural noise of victory comes out of him. The passion has increased ten fold; his hands are everywhere, searching my body eagerly. All I can do is stand there, his arse in my hands and hold on for dear life.

Pulling away from me, he looks into my eyes, as if trying to gauge if I will change my mind again, 'I promise to try to be gentle, and not to hurt you. If you are having second thoughts, say now, the minute we get upstairs, I don't think I'll be able to stop, even if you wanted me to.'

This scares me slightly, that his lust for me is so profound that he would struggle to stop; but it doesn't scare me enough to stop me from taking his hand and leading him back to the open doors of the dining room.

'Ah, Mi pequeno pajaro, you are my weakness' reaching down he picks me up, and carries me up the stairs, his lips are glued to mine.

Unbeknownst to us, our encounter in the garden has been witnessed by a pair of dark, jealous eyes. As soon as they were sure that we would not reappear, they left in search of someone, to tell all what they had seen.

Dismissing the guards at my bedroom door, Dalton kicks it closed with me still in his arms. Carefully placing me on my feet at the foot of my bed, he looks searchingly into my eyes, his gaze slowly working its way down to my mouth, a fleeting look of anger in his eyes, as his gaze rests on the imperfection caused by "Blondie."

With a voice full of emotion, he slowly says 'are you sure this is what you want? If you say no, then I will leave you alone, but, I must warn you; if you say yes, there is no going back; I will take everything you have to give, marking you as mine forever.'

I can't help but grin to myself that he is giving me the choice, I look into his eyes and witness a man fighting his internal demons.

'Decide' he is struggling with all of his might not to take what he wants from me; giving me the freedom to reject him if I wish.

In answer I stand on tiptoes, reach behind his head, and pull him down to kiss him gently on the lips.

Taking my lead he kisses me back just as gently; his mouth gently kissing each eyelid and the tip of my nose, before searching out my mouth once more. He reaches down and slowly removes my top, carefully pulling it over it my head, causing my hair to cascade down my back and over my face. Gently sweeping my hair back, he traces delicate kisses along my chin, down my neck and along each collarbone, the sensation mixed with my own arousal has me moaning and swaying into him, trying to deepen the touch.

Chuckling, he tells me, 'Mi pequeno pajaro, you are so beautiful, if only you knew what you do to me.'

His fingers are tracing circles on the back of my neck and along my hairline; gradually moving to the clasp of my bra, as he unhooks it and it drops to the floor. Moving his head towards my chest and exposed breasts he kisses the bud of a perfectly erect nipple, before sucking on it gently. His hands move to the fly of my jeans, unbuttoning and then unzipping them, pushing them, along with my underwear, gently to the floor. Looking into my eyes one final time before burying his head between my legs, placing a kiss on my most sensitive part; I gasp in shocked surprise.

Trailing small, feather-light kisses back up my abdomen; towards my breasts, he begins alternating between sucking and blowing on each nipple, causing each one to become even more erect, the cooling breeze making my areola form a circle of goose bumps, ecstatic at the effect his is having on them, he pulls each one into his mouth sucking hungrily.

Feeling underdressed, and wanting his rock-hard, naked body against me, I reach for his shirt, trying, and failing, to remove it, eager to run my hands over his muscular body. With a swift move he stands and begins to unbutton his shirt, as he undoes the last one, I reach underneath and shrug it off of his shoulders, relishing in the feel of his warm skin against my hands. Standing in front of me shirtless, he looks like a Greek Adonis, and I can't help but admire how toned and tanned he is. Compulsion makes me want to reach out and touch him, but as my hands move towards his bare chest, eager to feel his warmth and run my fingers between each muscular groove on his torso; he moves away from me; confused and hurt I look up at him.

'Mi pequeno pajaro, it is taking everything I have to control myself, and not to ravish you. I fear that if you touch me, I will loose control and hurt you. For now, just let me love you; when you are accustomed to me inside of you, you can touch me wherever you like. Ok?'

Nodding in agreement, thankful that he is being so considerate, I watch in eager anticipation as he continues to undress himself. His large erection springing to life from his boxers, as he slowly removes them, I cannot help but stare, and wonder how on earth that is going to fit inside of me, and become slightly worried that if he looses control; it may hurt a lot.

Dalton standing in front of me turns me around so that my back is pressed against him. I can feel the hardness of his cock resting on my pert buttocks. Moving my hair to one side, he peppers my neck and shoulder with slow gentle kisses, reaching his hands around me he begins to slowly caress my breasts; gently kneading, before pinching and pulling my nipples, the assault on my senses cause me to moan in pleasure. Placing a hand on my flat abdomen and pulling me even closer against him; I can feel his hot, rock-hard cock gyrating against my back. I moan in ecstasy, I cannot think anymore; only feel; the sensation of his mouth on my skin, his hands coaxing my nipples into stiff peaks, and his rock-hard cock on my back, making me gyrate my pelvis against, and in time with him; wanting and longing for him to be inside of me.

It never ceases to surprise me how quickly he can move; because before I know it I am laying on my back in the centre of the bed, with him on top of me; his cock so close to plunging deep inside of me. Unable to control myself any longer I lift my hips to meet his; begging for him to take me. This small movement has the opposite effect as he rears off of the bed, moving as quickly as possible away from me. Looking at him I can tell that he is fighting a war against himself; lying there naked and eager, I am secretly hoping that the demon in him wins this time.

Panther like, he comes back to lay above me, looking down into my eyes, with a veiled expression, excitement floods me, as I can see that the Demon has won.

'I warned you' is all he manages to say before he plunges his cock deep inside of me.

I scream so loud at the pain of being ripped open. He is so large that I can feel him hit the roof of my vagina with every painful thrust, filling and stretching me completely. The pain is so excruciating, I fear that I may pass out.

The speed and power with which he is thrusting into me

is forcing me up the bed. Adjusting our position, he kneels in front of my open legs, clasping my thighs in his hands pulling me back down onto him, continuing his powerful thrusts whilst holding onto my thighs, stopping my movement up the bed and away from him; I can feel him get deeper inside of me, the pain intensifying with each thrust.

Then gradually, my body becomes accustomed to the size of the cock that is now invading me, with all of its might. The pain gradually dissipates; and in its place is wave, upon wave of pure pleasure. With each thrust I can feel the raw power of him, I can feel my body relaxing, granting him deeper access, yearning for more. As if sensing a change in my body, he moves my feet over his shoulders, placing one of his hands either side of my head; he moves on top of me, looking down at me he slowly kisses each eyelid, his lips look wet when he looks in to my eyes again.

I hadn't realised that the pain from the initial primal thrusting had caused me to cry. Looking into my eyes, he slowly pulls his pulsating cock out, and then just as slowly pushes it teasingly back inside of me, over and over again.

With each slow thrust I begin to feel a tightening in my core, Dalton keeps to the same slow pace, looking into my eyes, waiting for a sign that my release is near. I can feel all of my muscles tightening, my vagina beginning to tighten and spasm; and as if on cue Dalton begins plunging deeper and faster into me, I am being forced up the bed, but am stopped as my shoulders meet with his hands. I feel the bed beneath me giving way with each powerful thrust. As he hits the roof of my vagina, the building tension is released with an orgasm so powerful, I can feel it behind my eyes. I can hear my heart pounding in my ears, beyond that I can hear the sound of my own voice, begging him to fuck me harder. He continues to pound into me, another orgasm quickly coming on the back of the previous one, over and over again, eventually I cannot tell when one orgasm ends, and the other begins. Still he doesn't stop thrusting into me, pile driving me into the bed; showing no signs of exertion, or of his own imminent release coming.

Eventually, I feel his cock growing in size inside of me, before hearing the guttural sound of his climax. I can feel his semen being pumped into my core, making me want more. Expecting him to pull his now flaccid cock out of me, I am shocked that he continues the same thrusting rhythm; taking me to the same dizzying heights of sexual bliss. My body feels like it's on an ever inclining roller coaster, waiting to hit the peak before coming crashing to earth. Dalton shifts his weight over me as he withdraws his cock; before I have time to react he flips me over onto all fours, penetrating even deeper inside of me. The new penetrating angle of this position makes his cock hit different areas inside of me. With every thrust, he pulls back on my hips, forcing himself even deeper inside of me. My vagina tightens around his cock again, as another orgasm rides on the back of the previous one. Feeling his cock begin to swell again, he pushes against my tightening flesh; quickening his pace, the weight of his balls hitting against my clitoris with each thrust, has me screaming his name. Hearing the roar signalling his second climax, I come crashing to earth with an almighty scream of ecstasy.

Exhausted, and gasping for air I collapse on my front, my whole body feels like jelly I feel the last orgasm chasing away. There is a pain between my legs that makes me wonder if I'll be able to walk in the morning. My mind is trying to make sense of what happened; I am no longer a virgin, I lost my virginity to Dalton Mercedes. I can't help feeling slightly ashamed that I would give my abductor the last piece of me, which was mine alone. But another part of me is elated that my first time was with such a sexual dynamo.

Feeling Dalton move I look over my shoulder and watch him as he lies next to me. Absentmindedly he begins tracing patterns with his fingers on my sweat licked back. With my nerve endings still hypersensitive from our fucking, it makes me moan in pleasure.

Before I know it Dalton is behind me again, pulling me back onto all fours. I can feel him inserting two fingers into my vagina, pumping them into my sore and tired flesh, which is soon forgotten as another orgasm takes hold. Continuing to pump hard into me with his two fingers, he slowly inserts another two fingers from his free hand, flexing and curling them inside me, causing them to graze against my g-spot. I can feel the pressure of another orgasm mounting, but not the kind of pressure from previously. Before I understand what's happening, the pressure releases, followed quickly by what I can only describe as a tap being turned on full blast, drenching both of us in a warm liquid.

Having no comprehension about what had just happened, and before I am able to make sense of it, and regulate my breathing, I feel Daltons rock hard cock slamming into me again. He is thrusting with such ferocity; he is like a caged animal, finally having a taste of freedom. Thrusting even deeper into me, mixing the pain of being stretched fully with an intoxicating sense of pleasure.

Placing his hands on my hips, he pulls me back towards

him with each thrust, making he thrusts slightly deeper, opening me wider, and trying to make my body accommodate his entire length. The pain is excruciating, I cry out in pain, begging him to stop. But when the relentless thrusting continues, I know that I have lost him and the Demon has taken full control again.

My arse stings as he strikes it hard, my skin stinging as he hits the same sensitive spot repeatedly. Trying to move away from his onslaught, he grips my hips tightly, pulling me back towards him. Pushing my face into the bed to muffle my screams, he continues the relentless pounding into me.

Holding me in place, I feel his hand lubricating my anus as he applies slight pressure with his thumb. Deep inside of me I am hoping that he doesn't mean to claim this part of me as well.

I scream in agony as I feel his thumb enter me, the pain unlike anything I had felt before. Slowly he moves his thumb deeper inside of me, until it hits the palm of his hand. Pulling it out entirely, before ever so slowly pushing inside of me again. The rhythm remains the same, slow thrusts with his thumb, whilst his cock continues to pound into me.

When he is satisfied that I have become accustomed to the sensation that I am feeling, he releases me from my prison, and moves the hand keeping my head in place on the bed to my clitoris. He begins gently massaging the area, whilst slowing the thrusting of his cock, keeping in time with the gentle invasion of his thumb inside of me.

For something that was initially so painful it now feels so right. I am in ecstasy; my mind has shut off, allowing my body to take control of what it needs. Rocking my hips backwards, forcing him deeper inside of me, I scream as I cum harder than before.

Dalton takes his cue from me and begins slamming into me with his cock; his thumb is no longer making long slow strokes, and is now matching pace with his relentless thrusting; the fingers on my over sensitised clitoris have become increasingly aggressive, rubbing harder and faster, forcing another orgasm out of my ruined body.

I feel Daltons rhythm change slightly as he cums quickly after me, chasing my orgasm with his own.

We collapse on the bed together, finally sated and exhausted. Sweat glistening on our bodies, unable to move or speak. Slowly drifting in to a peaceful sleep.

FOUR

I was woken the next morning by the smell of fresh coffee, and the sound of the ocean waves crashing on the shore, with the feel of a warm sea breeze drifting through the open doors. As I try to break through the fog of what happened last night and come to my senses, I look around the room, trying to place my whereabouts. Feeling a hard object prodding the small of my back, without thinking, I reach behind me, and grasp Daltons fully erect penis in my hand. As quickly as I grasp it I release it again; memories of last night come flooding back, and I feel the heat of embarrassment rising on my face.

I hear Dalton chuckling behind me, 'as much as I would like to carry on where we left off last night, but I have work to do,' turning me to face him, he leaves a passing kiss on my cheek, before standing and walking towards the bathroom.

Watching his perfectly formed backside walk away from me; I couldn't help but notice the scratch marks running down his back, and on his backside there were deep crescent shaped impressions that looked like nail imprints. Had I done that to him? Fearing that I may also be covered in scratch marks, or more bruises, I pull back the covers, and notice spots of deep red blood on the pristine white satin sheets. Checking that the stitches in my foot are still in place, I assume that the blood must have come from the scratch marks I had left on Daltons back and behind.

'I'll make Sophia run a bath for you, you could probably do with it after last night.' Sticking his head around the door, he notices me looking in confusion at the bloodstains on the bed. Winking at me, he says 'don't worry about the sheets, I'll have fresh put on for later.'

'I'm sorry if I hurt your back' I mumble, feeling the need to say something.

'No need to apologise, I enjoyed it. I did start to wonder if you had lied to me about being a virgin, but when I saw the blood …' a dark look flitted across his face as he remembered how rough he was with me last night, 'I tried to take it slow as soon as I realised, but when you squirted something took over me that I couldn't control.'

Walking towards me, he sat on the edge of the bed; cupping my head with one hand, and placing his other on my hip, 'I hope I didn't hurt you, I'm sorry if I did; but I can't guarantee that it won't happen again, you do things to me that I didn't know were possible' the look of lust in his eyes is apparent; making the mound between my legs throb and pulsate with longing.

Before I was able to confirm or deny if he had hurt me, my mouth was devoured in a hard kiss, devoid of passion. Beginning to kiss him back, hoping to ignite the same spark in him; he drew away, releasing me from his grip and walked back into the bathroom. I hear the definite click of him entering his adjoining room, leaving me with my confused thoughts. What was that all about? How can he turn his emotions off so quickly?

A soft knock at the door indicates that Sophia has arrived to run a bath for me, ridiculous really; I am perfectly capable to doing this for myself. Sophia enters smiling happily as she crosses the room, and enters the bathroom to begin the task at hand.

I hear the taps being turned on full as the bath is being prepared. The scent of soft floral tones wafts through the open door as Sophia liberally pours the bath crème into the hot running water, whilst humming distractedly to herself. Stretching under the sheets, a feel the tension from last nights exertions leave my body. Feeling unbelievably relaxed, I drift off, my mind replaying the surprising events of the previous evening. Still unable to believe that the animal Dalton works so hard to keep caged, was released by me and that I and actually enjoyed it when he lost control.

The sound of a phone ringing invades my thoughts and rouses me from my slumber; looking around the room, searching for a phone in the minimalist décor of my room. Curiosity makes me swing my legs out of the bed, and placing my feet on the floor, I stand and follow the direction the sound is coming from, I quickly realise that the sound is coming from behind the closed bathroom door, and suspecting that Dalton has returned, my heart skips a beat; eager to see him.

The need of having him inside me yet again is too strong to ignore. Approaching the bathroom door I can hear a female voice speaking perfect English, although a slight lilt of a Mexican accent is detectable. My curiosity gets the better of me, I had to know who this person is, who could speak fluent English; up to this point, the only person I am able to converse fully with is Dalton, and he is a man of little words. Expecting to see a member of Daltons staff that I hadn't yet met, and knowing that nearly fifty percent of the ones I had met are violent, I hesitantly reach for the handle to open the door, as my fingers seal around it, the door is pulled out of my grasp, being opened by whomever is inside.

The door swings open revealing Sophia standing there, with a mobile phone pressed close to her ear. Shock registers on her face, when her eyes meet mine, they quickly dart to the now empty bed and then back to me, it is perfectly apparent that she expected me to still be asleep. The colour drains from Sophias face, almost as quickly as the phone falls from her grasp, and crashes to the floor with a loud thud.

Recovering quickly, Sophia reaches down and picks up the phone, checking that it is not damaged before placing it in the pocket of her apron. "Miss, bath ready now' spoken in her usual broken English.

Realising that she is unaware that I was able to hear her speak perfect English, I decide to call her out on it. After all, it would make my time here so much more enjoyable if I am able to have a proper conversation with someone.

'Sophia, cut the bullshit! I heard you; I know that you can speak perfect English'

The colour drains from her face yet again; reaching for my arms with a vicelike grip she pulls me into the bathroom, making small shushing noises. Moving me to one side she locks the door behind me; placing her finger over her lips, she looks frantically at the adjoining bedroom door, before crossing the room to lock that one also. On her way back to join me she turns the shower on full, in a bid to drown out the noise coming from within.

'Ok, please don't tell him, please I'm begging you' Sophia is standing in front of me wringing her hands; she looks scared, desperate for her secret not to be revealed.

'Why? What difference would it make? Why are you so scared that Dalton shouldn't know?' unable to comprehend why she would need to keep this a secret, after all bilingual employees are usually seen as an asset.

'A few months ago, just after I began my employment here, he got word that there was an undercover DEA agent in his employee. All new employees were questioned; some intensely, which was tantamount to torture. I was cleared in the first round of questioning due to my inability to speak English fluently.'

'Did he find the agent?' although I had witnessed the demon lurking beneath Daltons posterior, I had trouble believing that he would torture his staff.

'No' Sophia looks imploringly at me, 'please you can not tell him, I would be sent for intensive questioning, he is still investigating all staff members; including those that he trusts implicitly, and that have been with him since the beginning'

The pathetic look on her face, and not wishing to be the cause of her being tortured, makes me cave; always a sucker for a sob story, 'ok, I won't say anything, I promise'

The look of relief shows on her face as she embraces me in a tight hug. If I wasn't completely naked, I would have hugged her back, but all I feel is a slight embarrassment; embarrassment along with a deep sense of concern, wondering what the consequences would be for me, should Dalton ever discover my part in her deception.

Realising my embarrassment, from my nudity and her embrace, she quickly releases me, 'oh Christ, sorry. Thank you so much for this, you're a lifesaver, I owe ya. I'll leave you to have a bath and I'll fetch you some breakfast, what do you fancy? Oh never mind, I'll bring you a selection. See you in your room in twenty minutes. Don't forget; Mums the word' her relief at my agreement to deceive Dalton is evident as she leaves the bathroom with a spring in her step.

Stepping into the hot bath water, a niggling feeling that I have made the wrong decision starts to surface in my mind. Have I made the right decision? Why did Sophia feel the need to lie to everyone? Who is the DEA agent that Sophia mentioned? Could it be her? Could they help me escape? Do I even want to escape now? What if Dalton finds out that I helped further Sophias subterfuge? Regardless of the questions I have, I will not find the answers lying in the bath. Deciding to track down Sophia and tackle this head on, I pull the plug out of the bath and stand to dry myself.

Wrapping a towel around my body and hair, I turn the off shower that Sophia had left on, and reach to unlock the door leading to Daltons bedroom. Feeling the prickly sensation that I only get when I'm in his presence, turning around, I see his body framed in the open door leading to my bedroom. With a dark look in his eyes he charges towards me.

'I had to see you' was all he managed to get out before crushing his lips to mine with a raw hunger.

I barely have time to draw breath before the towel is whipped away from my still damp body, my breast is in his mouth and his fingers are forced violently inside of me, his nails grazing the sensitive flesh at my core.

I am breathless, the raw hunger of his need driving me on to want more. Taking handfuls of his hair, I pull him away from my breasts, forcing his lips against mine, kissing him back with the same ferocity. We are lost in each other; our mouths glued together, seeking deeper contact. With his fingers thrusting deep inside of me, my release comes quickly, I cum screaming his name. Waiting expectantly, hoping to feel his hard cock pounding into me, a chill hits my bare skin; telling me that he is no longer holding me.

Looking down at me with a grin, 'something to remember me by' he turns on his heels and leaves.

Dazed and confused, I stumble into the dressing room to get dressed. My emotions are spiralling out of control, and my mind is trying to grasp any sense of normalcy. Despite the air-conditioned room, I can already feel the heat emanating from outside, feeling my usual attire of jeans wouldn't go well with my plans of visiting the garden after breakfast; I find a pair of white tailored shorts and team it with a white chiffon blouse.

As if on cue, I hear Sophias cheerful 'Miss, breakfast,' back to using broken English again, warning me that we must have company.

Leaving the dressing room, expecting to see Dalton waiting for me to join him for breakfast; I blanch as I come face to face with Blondie. The smile leaves my face, and I can feel the colour draining from it.

The look of pure anger in his eyes which spreads to the grimace on his face as he strides towards me. My fear of him, and the memory of the hard slap I had already received from him, has me recoiling away from him 'Un-fucking-believable' spittle leaving his mouth, and spraying my face, as he speaks. 'I had to see the whore for myself. Well, I hope you're enjoying this, because trust me it won't last.' Slamming the bedroom door behind himself as he leaves, I fall to the floor in a heap, shaking with anger and fear.

Sophia takes one look at the closed door before approaching me, whispering, 'Ell, are you ok? You need to be careful of Marcus, he has a nasty streak'

'Marcus?' my anger and fear of Blondie is making me confused. Who the hell is Marcus?

Helping me to my feet, Sophia nods towards the closed door, explaining, 'Marcus was a Navy Seal; he's seen a lot of conflict, which has left him with PTSD. Trust me, if you see him coming, run'

Sophia leads me to the balcony adjoining my room; the heat hits me instantly, and I am glad for my current clothing choice. The scene that greets me begins to make my mouth water almost instantly; a delicious array of fresh fruits, pastries and yoghurts are laid out on the table. It was enough to feed at least a dozen people; it felt criminal, knowing that most of it may go to waste, so I persuade Sophia to sit and eat with me.

Sophia was excellent company; although, despite using all of the questioning skills I have picked up as a Journalist, and several attempts at prodding I wasn't able to learn much about her, except that she was actually a lot older than I had originally thought. I decide that she must have been blessed with very good genes; aged 28 there were no signs of the lines you would expect to see on her flawless face.

When we have finished breakfast, I help Sophia clear the plates away, despite her fussing that I should leave them to her, and place them onto the trolley to be taken back to the kitchen. Deciding that now would be a good time to walk around the grounds, before the heat of the midday sun makes it unbearable, I begin to follow Sophia out of the room, the guards immediately stand in my path, blocking my exit.

'Miss, you stay. Senor Marcus, he say you stay'

Try as I might, I could not get passed the guards; it was like trying to push yourself through a brick wall.

'Am I a prisoner?' hoping upon hope that I am not.

'Yes' was all I heard, before one of the guards pushed me, full force, back into the room. I crash against the coffee table before falling on to the floor. The guard simply looked down at me, splayed out on the floor, pleased with what he had accomplished, laughing as he closes the door.

Picking myself up off the floor, I stand in shock, repeating to myself, 'I am a prisoner, what the fuck? I am a prisoner,' looking at the blood stains still on the bed, thoughts of the previous night and the incident that took place earlier in the bathroom, forced me re-evaluate the term "prisoner", 'I'm a sex slave' realisation dawns that Marcus was right, I am a whore.

With this realisation sinking in, I know that now, more than ever, I need to find a way to escape. I cannot, and will not, live my life being used and abused by Dalton, waiting to be disposed of when he tires of me.

Crossing to the balcony, I lean over and look down, trying to calculate the damage I would cause to myself if I were to simply jump. I could see a grassy area off to the right, but presumed trying to hit it would be impossible. Chuckling in remembrance at an old black and white film, which I watched as a child in one of my numerous foster homes; the prison inmates had made a makeshift rope out of sheets, looking at the bed, wondering if it is actually possible; I almost instantly discard the ludicrous idea. Number one; the guards would surely spot a makeshift rope, number two; if the rope didn't reach far enough to the ground, I could still cause some serious injuries.

Hearing the door open, I run back into the room; hoping to see Sophia back from taking the breakfast dishes to the kitchen. Telling me that it was all a big mistake, and that I am actually free to move around the grounds.

Marcus is standing there, as if the scar on his face wasn't scary enough, the look being thrown at me chilled me to the bone. Revelling in the apparent effect he was having on me, a smile that doesn't reach his eyes forms on his lips, 'you're coming with me.'

Fearing what he had planned for me I began backing towards the bathroom; thinking if I could make it there, I could lock him out.

As if sensing my plan, one word was all it took to stop me in my tracks, 'DON'T! You are coming with me whether you like it or not. We can do this the hard way or the easy way.' Looking at me as if undressing me with his eyes, 'please, make it the hard way. I would enjoy it so much more'

Realising that I had little choice, I could still feel the bruise from where he had hit me on the plane, I walk nervously towards him. As soon as I am alongside him, his hand reaches out, grabbing clumps of my hair and pulling my head back sharply.

'I hope Dalton tires of you soon, although considering what he suspects, it won't be long,' looking down at me with his face mere inches from mine, he looks down at my breasts which are clearly visible beneath my shirt. 'You need to be reconditioned, something I would love to do'

I am unable to move as he continues to leer at me, fear and panic is setting in and I pray that I find a way to escape before Dalton decides that he has had enough of me.

Marcus releases my hair, and moves his hand to tightly hold my arm; his fingers digging into my flesh. Dragging me through the house, the guards look away as they see him draw near; they are obviously as scared of him as I am.

'Sit, don't move' Marcus barks, as propels me to a small hard sofa; before walking through a door next to where I am sitting.

Listening carefully, I can hear a heated exchange between two men, one of them is definitely Marcus' and I am almost sure the second voice is Daltons.

'She's here'

'Fine' Daltons quipped tone resonates through the slightly ajar door.

'She should be at the cabin; not living it up like royalty'

'That is my decision to make, not yours'

'I'll take care of it, if you are to weak too'

I feel the wall behind me vibrate as the sound of glass smashes on the floor, before hearing 'GET THE FUCK OUT!'

Marcus yanks open the door; turning to look down at me I can see blood on his mouth; as if he had been punched, hard. 'You're making a mistake, you know who she is now. They'll be coming for her. Take my advice, send her away before it's too late.' Slamming the door, he gives me one final look of disgust, before skulking away.

I sit on the sofa; making myself as small as possible, whilst trying to stop my overactive imagination going into overdrive for whatever is coming next. What did he mean by "you know who she is now?" Even I do not fully know who I am, I only have vague memories of my childhood.

'Eloise, please come in' Dalton is standing in the

doorway, looking down at me, his face unreadable.

I can't help but notice that his term of endearment "little bird" has gone. What has happened to cause this dramatic change in him, making him so cold towards me after the passion we shared a few hours ago?

Walking into the room nervously, fearful that he is going to send me away and pass me around to his men; something he has threatened so many times, I avoid making eye contact with him. Looking around the room I notice that the monochrome pallet has been replaced with a pallet of black and red. Dalton steers me towards a large, black gloss desk, which sits at the end of the room; two chairs sit opposite as if a meeting were about to take place. I walk past two black leather sofas, which are facing each other with a coffee table in between them; all sitting on a blood red carpet. Seating me on one of the chairs, Dalton moves to the other side of the desk; I now realise that this room is his office.

Relaxing back into his chair, he picks up a pen and begins turning it between his fingers. Staring at my face assessing my reactions, he begins 'Who is Eduardo Mendez to you?'

'Eduardo who?' Confusion hits, it is evident that he thinks that this name should mean something to me, but I am sure that I haven't heard it before.

'Don't play games with me. My tech team have taken your laptop apart, and have found photos of Eduardo Mendez on it. Answer the question, who is Eduardo Mendez to you?' the anger boiling underneath the surface is apparent, making me recoil in my seat, trying to get as much distance as possible between us.

'Dalton, I don't know who you mean. I have never heard

of this person, and I don't know how his photo got onto my laptop' I can hear my voice pleading with him. I begin racking my brain, trying to figure out who could have planted it on my laptop. As far as I can remember, no one has the password; or would even have had access to my laptop to enable this.

Dalton opens a brown manila folder on his desk; leaning forward he begins to place pictures on the desk in front of me; pictures of my father. Confused I look into Daltons black eyes.

'This is Eduardo Mendez' with each word he stabs a finger on each of the photos, without looking away from me.

'No, no this is a mistake. This man is Edward Mansell; he is my father' looking pleadingly into his eyes, hoping that he can see that I am telling the truth, and that this is all just a big misunderstanding.

Dalton sits back, a grin of delight on his face; as if he already knew this information. 'Well haven't I caught a pretty little bird, none other than the daughter of my greatest adversary. What to do with you now?' musing over his options aloud; 'I could cut little pieces off of you and mail them back to daddy dearest; I could let my men do every depraved thing to you and send your dear papa a video; or I could keep you here, my own little bird in a gilded cage. What to do? What to do?'

Stunned into silence, reeling from this obvious case of mistaken identity, I sit frozen. My father wasn't a criminal; he was a banker, and he certainly wasn't this "Eduardo Mendez" character either. He was also dead, very, very dead. Looking at Dalton; lost in thought, I got the impression that he had forgotten all about me sitting opposite him, I reach across the table to touch his hand, trying to reconnect with him on a physical level. Seeing my movement he snatched his hand away, as if afraid that my touch would burn him.

'Marcus, come here'

I hear the heavy footsteps of Marcus as he enters the room, 'well? Did she confess?'

Again, both of them are ignoring my existence. Looking from one to the other, searching for a sign of what my fate was to be.

'Yes, you were right. Get her out of my sight. You know where to put her' Dalton refuses to look at me as he stands and walks to the window. Looking out at the sea view as if my existence has already been forgotten.

Marcus snaps his fingers, and two burly guards come into the room, their weapons hanging at their hips, with a smaller pistol tucked into a shoulder holster. Quickly approaching me, giving me no time to think, they grasp each arm and pull me sharply out of the chair, to my feet.

Tears stream down my face as I plead with him, 'Dalton, please, listen to me. My father is Edward Mansell, he was a banker in London, and he's dead, he was murdered, along with my mother, when I was a child. I grew up in care afterwards, check it; please just check it. Please, I beg of you, please listen to me.'

My pleas fall onto deaf ears. He was lost to me. My legs crumble beneath me, and I feel a stabbing pain in my chest, as if my heart is breaking. The guards, unfazed by my outburst, continue dragging me towards the open office door, my shoes being removed in the process, causing carpet burns to my heels.

'Dalton' screaming his name, hoping to snap him out of whatever trance he is in.

Dalton barely acknowledges me; a swift glance in my

direction tells me that his demons have once again taken over. I am being dragged, pleading, out of his office, while he merely turns his back on me, continuing to admire the view in front of him.

Still screaming Daltons name, as I am bundled into a waiting jeep; hoping to break through the cold exterior he has placed around his self. A guard sits either side of me on the back seat, the sheer bulk of their frame leaving little space for me; I am wedged in so tight that a seatbelt is not required. Marcus gets into the drivers seat and starts the engine. Before putting the car into gear, he reaches behind and grabs my face with his thumb and forefinger, squeezing hard, and forcing my mouth open.

'Shut up you bitch, or I will make you,' shouting with pure venom in my direction. He releases me, and I feel fresh bruises starting to form.

I instantly stop shouting for Dalton, my breath coming in on sobs of pain and fear. I look behind at the house as we speed out of the gates, hoping that Dalton has changed his mind; hoping to see him run after me, and reclaim me as his. I continue to watch until the white house is nothing but a speck in the distance. My heart sinks even deeper as I realise that he obviously doesn't care; I am now nothing more than a pawn in his vendetta against "Eduardo Mendez" whoever the hell that is. The smooth tarmac road soon gives way to a bumpy dirt track; I am jostled about between the two guards, causing even more bruises. The cut on my lip is beginning to throb, probably caused by Marcus' recent manhandling me; tentatively I touch it, looking at my hand I see the redness of my blood, the same red as Daltons office carpet, I silently weep.

The journey to wherever it is that I am being taken seems

to take forever, and the further away from Dalton I am taken, the stronger the stabbing pain in my chest gets. I need to speak with him, to reason with him, and to make him see that this is all a misunderstanding. I have to see him, just once, just to see if he is hurting as much as me. If he isn't, then at least I'll know where I stand, I can then formulate a plan to escape.

Feeling the car slow to a stop, I look out of the windows. What greets me I can only describe as a prison; a 10-foot wire fence surrounds the perimeter, topped with rolled barbed wire, with guard towers spaced at regular intervals, each one manned by two armed guards. Escape was looking virtually impossible at the moment.

One of the guards on the gate puts his head through the open window, greeting Marcus, and he looking at me, 'this her?'

'Yep, this is the one you've heard about. You know the drill. Where do you want me to put her?'

'Section 6 has room, put her there.'

'Is that where Esme is? I've missed her, I may just pay her a visit while I'm here'

Chuckling the guard says 'you old goat, I'm sure she's missed you too' leering at me, while licking his lips, he continues, 'have fun boys'

Marcus continues to drive further into the compound. Looking around I can see about twenty large log cabins, there are women of various ages sitting on the porches. Washing lines are strung between them, with fresh laundry drying in the soft breeze. It reminded me of a concentration camp, although the women didn't look malnourished, and I could hear the sound of children playing noisily in the distance. What on earth is this place?

The car pulls up at one of the cabins in the centre of the compound, putting the car into neutral, and pulling on the handbrake, Marcus switches the engine off.

Turning in his seat to face me 'Welcome to the Cabin. There are a few rules for you to follow whilst you enjoy your stay here; if any man visits you, they are expected to pay, you will give ten percent of your earnings to your block guard, to pay towards your bed and board. Follow these simple rules and you will be treated with respect. Failure to follow these rules will result in your death.'

Seeing realisation dawn on my face; that I am now expected to become a prostitute, or I will be executed, all because of a case of mistaken identity, he laughs.

'Don't worry, no one will touch you until your wounds have healed, no one will want some one as ugly as you look right now. Once word gets around whom your father is, I think you will be one of the best-paid whores here. A lot of the men will do anything to get back at him.'

Marcus exits the car and one of the women rushes up to greet him; he embraces her in a hug full of warmth, before she leads him into the cabin. Feeling a tug on my arm, I notice that the guards have also left the car, and one of them is trying to pull me out. Having no wish to be left here, I refuse to move. The guard, losing his patience, reaches in and grabs my hair, using it to pull me out, depositing me heavily on the hard ground. Some of the older women; looking on me with pity, come to my aid and help me to my feet, shouting at the guard for causing me further injuries.

Speaking in Spanish, I can only assume what he was telling them. But if I had to guess, it would be that my father was supposedly "Eduardo Mendez" A lot of the women's faces change from pity to anger and hatred, a few even spit at me whilst shouting "Puta". Standing in shock, unable to understand what was being said about or to me, I begin to sob uncontrollably.

The eldest woman, speaking harshly in Spanish, shoos them away. Looking at me, she pulls a tissue from her pocket, and carefully dabs at the tears flowing from my eyes, speaking in Spanish the whole time, all I can do is look at her dumbly, unable to understand what she is saying to me.

'Thank you' was all I could manage between my sobs.

'Are you American?'

'No, I'm English.'

'English? I once went to England; I'd like to go back there one day. I'm Marcella, by the way'

'Hello Marcella, I'm Eloise, pleased to meet you. Thank you for helping me'

'Don't mention it. Don't worry about the girls, they'll soon calm down. You're father is a very bad man, most of us are here because of him.'

'I know what Dalton thinks, but he is wrong, my father isn't this Eduardo everyone hates so much. My father was a banker. He was killed when I was eight. I don't understand what is happening here. I have to see Dalton, I have to make him listen to me.'

'I wouldn't hold your breath sweetheart, He never comes here anymore, occasionally one of us is selected to visit him, but never for very long. Mostly the men come, some of us have our regulars; we are well treated, and we get to raise our children, a few of the women are even married to some of the men on the

Island. We are kept safe from people like your, I mean, like Eduardo. It's a good life '

'But this is a prison.'

'It wasn't; yes, the fencing has always been there, along with the guard towers, but the guards? They're new; they arrived just before we got word of your arrival. The guards? They're here for you.' With this she took my arm and led me into the cabin.

Marcella shows me where the shower room and kitchen is; opening the cupboards she shows me which area in each is mine. Telling me that Senor Mercedes will take care of the provisions for me until I am able to work. Leading me into another room, informing me that it is my quarters, she leaves me to 'get settled'. The room is small; consisting of a double bed, a dressing table, and a wardrobe; not that I have any clothes to put in my wardrobe, there is a small sink in the corner of the room, with a small mirror above it. Everything is drab and grey; I can't help feeling that the room perfectly matches the way that I am currently feeling.

I am still reeling from everything that has happened since breakfast. How could things have changed so quickly? I woke this morning feeling a lot happier than I do right now. I curl up on the bed and cry until there is no more tears coming, and then my body begins to tremble in fear.

I can hear the noises of lovemaking in the room adjoining mine. The sound makes me feel sick, as I know that soon I will suffer the same fate. I can hear the woman screaming in ecstasy; somehow, I don't think that I will be able to fake it so well.

Placing the pillow over my head, to drown out the noises, I fall into a fitful sleep.

The following few days are spent with me laying on the bed and staring at the ceiling, through tear-stained eyes; reliving my last encounter with Dalton. The hatred in his eyes still haunts my every waking hour, the nightmares that come as soon as I close my eyes are even worse. Making me wake in a cold sweat and screaming his name.

In my dreams I see him in the distance, the faster I run towards him, the further away he appears. If I do manage to reach him, he does not see or hear me, I stand in front of him; pounding my fists on his chest, screaming his name. Each night I wake in a cold sweat, with Marcella gently stroking my face, trying to rouse me from the nightmare that has taken hold.

After the third night, Marcella quickly realised that as soon as sleep takes me, the nightmares would begin. She began sleeping next to me, rocking me like a child, hoping her presence and the comfort she gave would rescue me from the darkness.

Each morning she brings a selection of fresh fruits and sweet pastries; leaving them on the table next to my bed, along with a cup of fresh coffee; at lunchtime the untouched plates are removed, replaced by another meal; which will remain untouched. The same routine is carried out at dinnertime. Unable to eat, I look at the food with disgust, before turning away from it. Despite Marcella trying to tempt me to eat and drink, nothing that is put in front of me is appetising enough to persuade me to eat.

I am only leaving my room to use the facilities in the shower room; standing under scalding hot water, and using a nailbrush I scrub at my skin, trying to force myself to feel something again. Causing grazes all over my body, which in the heat quickly become sore and infected. Changing into fresh clothing, that was brought from the house for me; I enter my room and collapse on the bed, exhausted from my efforts, my body weak from the lack of food and fluid.

After nearly two weeks Marcella becomes increasingly concerned about my welfare. After I develop a fever she sends for the doctor to visit me, I am too weak to tell her not to bother, and that I would rather die than live a life like this.

When Pedro arrives, Marcella quickly follows him into my room; I barely acknowledge their presence. Pedro speaks in hushed tones with Marcella, whilst looking at my fragile form with concern, before plastering a smile on to his face and approaching me.

'Elly, Pedro would like to take your temperature, your blood pressure and listen to your chest. Is that ok?'

Nodding my confirmation, Pedro places a thermometer beneath my tongue; removing it a short time later, after looking at the reading his self, he shows it to Marcella who clicks her tongue in frustration. As he begins to roll up one of the sleeves of my blouse to take my blood pressure, he stops when he sees the infected red marks on my skin, caused by my overzealous scrubbing in the shower. Marcella walks to the other side of the bed, and pulls back the bed covers; she carefully begins to remove my clothing, inspecting the severity of what I have done to myself. They are both shocked to discover that there is barely an inch of undamaged skin.

Pedro angrily shakes his head, stands and leaves the room. Unable to believe, that someone would inflict so much pain on their selves.

Marcella carefully places the covers back over me, afraid of causing more damage to my fragile skin, before following

Pedro out. I can hear them talking in the hallway outside of my room; Marcella sounding angry, Pedro sounding resigned. Hearing their footsteps fading into the distance, I lie completely still, waiting for the nightmares that sleep will soon bring with it.

Marcella is back before sleep takes hold, which I am thankful for. She has been a great comfort to me, and has never left my side. When she enters my room, she looks so angry with me, 'what have you done to yourself? If you want to die, I will not help you. Well do you?'

Looking up at her in confusion, my brain being starved of nutrition is struggling to keep up.

'Do you want to die?'

'I don't know' I answer as honestly as I can, until this moment in time; I hadn't really given much thought to my future. Do I really want to die? Do I want to accept the situation I now find myself in, or do I want to find a way out? In truth, no, I don't want to die. No, I will not accept my situation, and I will find a way to escape. 'No, Marcella, I don't want to die.'

'Then eat, start to look after yourself, I cannot be here constantly looking over you'

'You're right, I'm sorry, I promise I'll try harder.'

Relieved that I have made a decision, and sensing a change in my resolve; Marcella leaves the room. I can hear her in the kitchen preparing some food, and deciding that now is as good a time as any to begin repairing myself, I follow the sound to the kitchen.

As I approach the open door, I can hear lots of chattering, but as soon as I enter the room, there is silence, you could hear a pin drop. Around the large wooden table there are four women, some of them have babies on their laps, whilst toddlers are playing tag, chasing each other around the table. The women look at me with distaste, the anger and hatred they are feeling towards me is apparent.

'She is not responsible for her fathers actions, and she will not be held accountable' Marcella tells the women, before turning to me smiling, 'Elly, it's good to see you out of your room, take a seat and I'll bring you something to eat.'

Seeing my reservations about sitting with the women who so clearly despised me, she gave them one look, before looking back at me with a smile.

'Don't worry about them; they'll come round to you. Please don't blame them for their reaction towards you; your father was the man responsible for trafficking and enslaving them. Most of them still bear the mental scars from their ordeal'

'My father is dead' I can't help feeling appalled for the way these women have been treated, but they need to understand that my father wasn't responsible. He was a good man and showered me, and my mother, with affection. He could not hurt anyone even if he wanted to.

'I'm sorry to break it to you, but, Eduardo is very much alive'

'Eduardo is not my father. My father was murdered when I was eight, along with my mother.'

'Did you not tell Senor Mercedes that the photo on you laptop was of your father?'

'Yes, I did, but his name is Edward, not Eduardo'

'Elly, I'm sorry, but the photo is of Eduardo, you have been lied to. Your father is alive, I do not know anything of your mother.'

Hearing the sound of cars pulling up outside, the women

excitedly grab their children and run towards the front door, with one of the toddlers running ahead of their mother, shouting 'papa'. The car doors are slammed shut, and I can hear children giggling as their fathers swoop them into the air. Feeling slightly jealous at their happiness; wondering if I will ever feel anything again, I rise from the table to return to my room. Before I am able to turn towards the kitchen door, I feel him; Dalton is here. I collapse at the table and avert my eyes away from him, trying to make myself as small as possible so that he does not notice my presence.

'Senor' the only discernable word I am able to understand, before they begin their conversation in rapid Spanish. I can feel his eyes on me the whole time, willing me to look in his direction. When they have finished speaking the silence is deafening, I can feel two pairs of eyes burning into the back of me. Marcella crosses the kitchen, and places a comforting hand on my shoulder, 'Senor would like to speak with you. I will be outside if you need me'

In my mind, I reach out to her, holding on to her for dear life, pleading with her to stay, not wishing to be left alone with him. But as I hear her footsteps leave, I realise that I have only pleaded with her in mind, and I am now alone with him.

Afraid I will make a bolt for it, he stands in the kitchen door, assessing how best to deal with me. As if coming to a decision, he kicks the door closed, and drags a chair to sit opposite me. Out of the corner of my eye I see his hands move along the table towards mine, as if reaching out to hold them, I quickly withdraw them and place them on my lap out of harms way.

'Elly, I'm sorry. I had to know, I needed time to find out

the truth. Please can we talk about this? I swear no one would have harmed you.'

I do not move, I do not speak, and I daren't look in his direction for fear of crumbling, and succumbing to the lust that is already rearing its ugly head.

'Elly, please, I am miserable without you.'

He tries unsuccessfully to get a response from me. Eventually seeming to decide to give up; he stands from the table and moves towards the door.

'Marcella, can you pack Ellys things and put them in Marcus' Jeep, I'm taking her home with me'

I try to respond, to tell him that I would rather die than spend another minute in his company.

Taking my silence as acceptance, he swoops me up in to his arms; holding me close, we walk through the building to his waiting car. Bundling me into the back, he swiftly gets in to the car behind me, holding me close as we begin the drive back to the mansion, repeating quietly 'I'm sorry' and tenderly kissing my head.

When we arrive there is no welcoming reception as I previously witnessed. There are no guards stationed on the front door. Perhaps he is ashamed of the repercussions of his actions, and he does not wish his men to witness the state that I am now in. Dalton carries me inside the cool exterior, occasionally I can feel his eyes on my face, I refuse to look at him, I cannot look him.

Carrying me away from the main staircase of the house, and through a labyrinth of doors at one end of the house, he gently places me on the floor in a room that is a direct contrast from the rest of the masculine interior that I had seen so far.

Everything is this room is white; white floors, white furniture, white walls, and white lace curtains hanging at the two sets of glazed patio doors. It has a very feminine feel, and I can't help thinking that he must have had some help with this.

There are two high back armchairs, placed at an angle to each other, in front of one of the open doors; the perfect position to take in the views of the ocean. A small glass coffee table is placed in the space between the two chairs and the doors. A selection of English gossip magazines on display. Vases of freshly cut flowers fill each of the surfaces; looking at them reminded me of the ones I spotted in his garden after dinner, on that fateful evening.

Without taking his eyes off of me, he crosses the room to a sideboard, picking up a decanter; he pours two large glasses of a strong smelling spirit. Indicating for me to sit in one of the chairs, he offers one of the glasses to me.

Mutely taking it, I sit at the proffered seat, and wait for him to speak. Grasping my last ounce of courage; when the silence becomes too much to bear, I look up at him, 'well? What do you want from me now?' said with more force than I felt.

He looks at me, the hurt showing in his eyes, 'I do not want anything from you. I am sorry that I sent you away; it is a decision that I will regret for the rest of my life. Before I can ask you to forgive me, perhaps I should explain things.' he takes a mouthful of the spirit in his glass, draining the contents; and picking up the decanter before sitting on the seat opposite me, 'how much do you know of my family and their ties with Eduardo Mendez?'

Deciding against drinking the spirit in my glass, I place it on the table between us, and push it away. 'I know a little of your family, and until recently I had never heard the name Eduardo Mendez'

Taking another slug of the spirit, he continues, 'in that case, I'd best start at the beginning. My father and yours; whether you want to believe it or not, Eduardo is your father, were friends; best friends. Between them they took over, and organised smaller businesses, eventually they became the biggest import and export company in the world. Their names became well known, they were respected globally, known to be firm but fair and they treated all of their staff well. Everything was going great, until one day my father discovered that yours had gotten greedy, he had begun a side operation; trafficking and enslaving women, selling them to brothels, or the next highest bidder. My father loved women, all women, no matter of their size or age; all of my fathers men knew that women and children were not to be harmed during any takeover operation. The thought of what your father was doing to them disgusted him, and without thinking of the repercussions, he confronted your father; who denied it all of course. Faced with the evidence, things got violent and he was sent packing with his tail between his legs. My father made it known that Eduardo was no longer involved with the business anymore, and anyone found to be helping him would be severely punished. Thinking that this was the end of it, we settled back into our everyday lives. A year later, your father came calling, whilst my father was away; he stormed the home where we were living, killing the guards, before kidnapping my mother and myself; she later died from the injuries they inflicted on her; my father never saw her alive again. After my mothers death, your father went underground, eventually trying to fake his own death, but he asked the wrong people for help; after questioning, they squealed like pigs. What no one was aware of, however, was of your existence; he managed to keep you a secret for all of these years.'

'I am sorry for everything that has happened to you and your family, I am so sorry for the loss of your mother; but that man is not my father' I am sorry, I feel it in my heart, I am sorry that he was kidnapped, I am sorry that his mother was murdered, but how can I make him see that that man is not my father.

'But he is,' placing a note on the table 'this arrived here the very same day that you did.'

I pick it up to read it.

"Give back what you have taken from me; I know you have her. Give back my daughter. If you harm her, there will be a war. Eduardo."

'We were uncertain of who he meant, that is until you confirmed that the picture of him was your father.'

I drop the note as if it would burn me, how can this be? How can my father, who I loved so dearly, be this monster everyone keeps telling me about? It isn't possible.

'Elly, you are safe here, I won't let him, or anyone else for that matter, hurt you' crouching on the floor next to me, he takes his hands in mine, rubbing his thumb over my now healed wrists.

'Why would he hurt me? Why would anyone want to hurt me? If he is my father, he would never hurt me' I am adamant that my father is a good man, I will not let any of these strangers convince me otherwise, almost certain that he must love me as much as I loved him, and he would never truly hurt me.

'Elly, your father has changed a lot over the years. I have no doubt that he would sell you to the highest bidder; all he cares about is money. And, well, other people will want to hurt you, to hurt me.'

Hurt him? How could someone harming me possibly affect or hurt him? He has obviously had too much to drink.

'Elly, there is a spy here; probably more than one. Someone has reported back to your father about how much they suspect that you mean to me; if your father knows, you can bet your bottom dollar, that the other families also know. We were witnessed in the garden, before I made you mine. Unknowingly I have placed you in great danger'

'How much I mean to you? Are you nuts? You hardly know me'

'That isn't entirely true, I have been following you for a while; I know how you like your coffee, what you like for breakfast, that you are too busy trying to become a serious reporter, so that you do not take care of yourself properly; microwave meals every night for dinner is not very good for you. The dimples that are created in your cheeks when you smile have been cemented on my mind.'

The only way that he could know this information about my habits is if he had been following me for sometime, internally kicking myself that I hadn't even noticed that I was being watched.

'Imagine my delight when I arrive at my club to audition some dancers and see you working at the bar. It felt like all of my Christmases and birthdays rolling into one; the journalist who was hell bent on bringing down my empire, was working undercover at my establishment.' Chuckling to himself at the memory of this, he continues, 'what could I do? I was curious at how far you would take your alternate ego, and how hungry you were for the story. So I sent all of the prospective dancers home, with a hefty sum of money to thank them for the inconvenience caused, and made some of the bar staff would prefer to be dancers audition instead; a lot of them were very happy with this arrangement as the men tend to tip them a lot better. I was delighted when you continued to play your part; I knew in that moment that I had to have you'

'You knew I was a journalist the whole time?'

'Yes, of course, I didn't realise that you were working for me until that night, but I knew you were a journalist. I am curious how you came to be working undercover there though.'

'I had a tip off that girls were going missing from the club, and that it could be linked to the sex trafficking case I was investigating'

'Who is your source? Girls are not going missing from my club, if they were, I would know about it' his voice is like thunder, the thought that girls could be going missing from his club, whilst under his protection, filling him with rage.

I can feel his temper flaring, and decide that if I tell him everything that I know, it may have the desired effect of calming him down.

'I can't tell you who it is' holding my hand up, asking him to wait before he explodes, 'it was an anonymous tip off, posted through my door one night. It had names of people I should pursue, written statements from women who had supposedly been rescued. Along with a list of buildings, and properties of interest; all of it pointing back to you.'

'When was this?' his mind clearly calculating a time line of events.

'I don't know, eighteen months, two years maybe.'

'Interesting, that is about the same time that I was made aware of you.'

Standing, deep in thought, as if struggling to control his emotions, he reaches down and moves a stray hair from my face, 'Mi pequeno pajaro, all I want to do is hold you and take away the hurt I have caused, but I know I have a long way to go before you can forgive me' he drops his hand away from me dejectedly, and begins to walk out of the door, pausing briefly he turns, fixing me with his full attention 'this apartment was my mothers; I hope that you will find it comfortable. I will send Sophia to take care of your needs' a quick bow of his head and he's gone.

FIVE

The revelations from our conversation are replaying in my mind; my father is alive, does this also mean that my mother is alive? My thoughts are in conflict with each other, as much as I want to find them, and ask them why they left me, I am also waking up to the realisation that my father is a monster. Could it be that this is all his doing? Placing the tip off under my nose, knowing that I was green and eager enough to follow it through, without thinking about the consequences, also knowing that Dalton would come looking for me when he was wrongly informed of the truth behind my investigation. Did my father realise the trauma he would cause me? The man that I knew and loved, and that I called Daddy growing up, was not capable of such things; but this other man? Without any doubt, I believe that he would be capable of anything. In my heart, I also know deep down that my mother is dead, and my father is the one who killed her.

Lost in my thoughts, churning over every small piece of information I can remember, I am startled when a hand is placed on my shoulder. I was concentrating so hard, I didn't hear Sophia enter the room or call my name.

'Miss, you ok?'

Looking up at her, I see the look of sadness in her eyes when she takes in my appearance; she quickly crosses to the door, closes and locks it. Without even having time to blink, she has practically picked me up out of the chair into a tight hug.

'Oh Ell, what have you done to yourself? You were already thin, but now you look like a famine victim.' Releasing me, she holds me at arms length, looking at me properly for the first time in nearly two weeks.

'I couldn't eat' I choked out on small sobs of relief at seeing a friendly face.

'How did you do this to your skin' she lifts up the sleeves of my top, looking at the red marks underneath.

I look down at them, as if seeing them for the first time; remembering how I had scrubbed at my skin so hard, trying desperately to feel something. Shocked at the damage I have inflicted on myself, but unable to admit to myself or anyone else why I did it, I simply reply, 'I don't know'

Sophia held me in another embrace, before guiding me through the apartment. Everything was white, except for small accents of pale pink; either in a light, an ornament or woven into one of the deep pile rugs. There was another sitting room; this time with velvet covered sofas, pink scatter cushions and a plush deep pile rug, all of the furniture was white, with another set of double doors led to the gardens outside. There was a well-appointed kitchen, a large dining room with seating for ten people, a guest bathroom and two bedrooms with en-suites. All in the same white pallet with pale pink accents, it had a very calming effect on me; it made me think of heaven on earth.

Sophia leads me into the largest of the two bedrooms; in the middle of the far wall stands the largest bed I have ever seen; I wasn't even sure that it was a standard size, you could fit three people spread-eagled comfortably on it, and it is so high that the mattress comes to my waist, the en-suite had a two person bath, a large walk in shower, two sinks side by side, and a sauna in the far corner. There are three sets of double doors which lead out into the garden, I try the handle of one of them, expecting it to be locked, and am pleasantly surprised when it opens. Stepping through the opening I notice two armed guards standing either side of it; I stand on the threshold waiting for them to push me back inside of the room, when it doesn't come, I take one hesitant step outside whilst still waiting for the forceful nudge.

Sophia coming behind me takes my hand and leads me outside, 'is ok miss,'

We are standing in an enclosed private garden, surrounded by a large hedgerow; flowerbeds full of brilliant coloured blooms in every direction I look. As I look around, I notice the sheer amount of guards dotted around for my protection; there are two on each door leading to the room we have just exited. Occasionally I can spot a head bobbing above the hedge line, which makes me think that there must be some form of walkway behind it. With so many guards; I am clearly still a prisoner, albeit a prisoner who is being kept in luxury; a bird in a gilded cage.

I can tell that Sophia is becoming excited as she drags me around the side of the building. As soon as I pass the corner I could understand why; a swimming pool and a hot tub greet me. There are wooden sunbeds surrounding the pool, along with large pots filled to bursting with fragrant flowers. At the far end of the pool there is a summerhouse, along with more guards. It appears that although I am able to move freely in the garden, my every move will be monitored.

Sophia pulls me back inside the apartment through

another set of open doors, we are in another bedroom, smaller than the last but still large none the less, there is a super king sized bed, with a small armchair near the open doors. 'My room,' grinning from ear to ear, she spins on the spot, as if she can't believe her luck. Pointing at the larger bedroom across the hall, 'your room'.

Feeling her excitement, I hug her swiftly, secretly pleased that I have a room mate; I have been living on my own for far to long. Having some female company could be good for me. Suddenly feeling very tired; the shock of discovering who my father actually is, along with the excitement of having a housemate, is beginning to take its toll. I politely ask 'Sophia, do you mind if I go to bed? I am exhausted.'

Closing the doors leading to the outside to drown out our voices, she hugs me quickly, 'no not at all, you look dead on your feet. I'll arrange for your things to be brought down and put them in your dressing room, there is a second door leading into the hallway so you won't be disturbed.'

I can't help feeling how considerate she is, possibly my only friend in this place, but as soon as the thought enters my head I feel ashamed, as Marcella had been so good to me during my time at the cabin.

'Thank you, that's very kind of you.'

'Oh, one last thing; I forgot to show you the panic alarms. Around the apartment you will see lots of these switches,' pointing to a red switch on the wall, and some next to the bed, I look around the room and I count ten in total; now that they have been pointed out to me, I couldn't believe that I had previously missed them. 'If anyone that you do not recognise tries to approach you, press the button. Your guards will be with you in seconds. I will introduce you to your personal guards later, only these men are allowed near you. They have been strictly vetted and are Senors best men.'

'Really? That's a bit extreme, why the need for all the security? It's not as if I am going to get far'

'I can't tell you that, but I'm sure when he is ready, he will let you know.' Shooing me out of her room, 'Go, sleep, I will take care of everything. Any special request for dinner, you look as if you could do with something to eat.'

'Thank you, I honestly don't think I could eat anything, but I promise you that I will try.'

I don't remember walking the short distance to my room, or getting into the comfortable bed, as soon as my head hit the pillow I must have fallen fast asleep.

My nightmares are still there, but this time they have changed; I am a little girl again, I can hear glass breaking and screaming coming from downstairs; my mother is screaming, pleading with someone. I can hear lots of men shouting, before the sound of a gun firing. I am hiding under the bed in my parents' bedroom. The sound of footsteps on the stairs are coming closer to my hiding place. The wailing of a police siren outside makes the footsteps run in the opposite direction, before leaving my home. I slowly come out from underneath the bed; walking down the stairs in search of my parents; at the foot of the stairs I see my mothers body, covered in blood; with a gunshot wound in her back. I can just make out the feet of my father leading into the kitchen, approaching him I catch a glimpse of his face, but before I can get too close I am bundled into the arms of a police officer.

A sharp slap around my face breaks me from my

nightmare; but I had seen enough to know that this was not a nightmare; it was a memory. The memory of the night my parents were supposedly murdered; except that the dead man that was lying there was not my father.

Sophia is standing over me, 'so sorry, you not wake'

'He's alive, he wasn't murdered' was all I managed to say before I start sobbing uncontrollably. Sophia holds me close, waiting for the tears to subside.

Behind her I spot six guards, with their weapons raised, checking the room for invaders, while Dalton is standing at the foot of my bed, his hands gripping the footboard so tightly his knuckles were turning white, seeming unsure if he should approach me or not.

'Sophia leave us,' Dalton looking at the guards 'you lot too, all of you, out now'

Everyone follows his command and leaves the room; he walks to the far side and resets the silent panic alarm that Sophia must have pressed when she was unable to rouse me. He slowly turns to look at me; now propped up in bed, my sobbing having subsided to embarrassment that my nightmare has caused such a commotion. Dalton walks back to the foot of my bed and places his hands on the footboard, as if waiting for me to speak.

'I'm sorry to cause such a problem. I had a nightmare that's all.' Not yet able to admit to myself, or divulge the fact that I am almost certain it was a memory from my childhood.

Clamping his jaw tightly, I can see the muscles working as a grim look of concern spreads across his face, 'was it the same one that you have been having all week?'

How did he know I had been having nightmares? The only person who knew would be Marcella.

'Marcella kept me informed of your wellbeing,' he confirmed. Grimacing at the memory of the pain that he has inflicted on me, 'I'm sorry for my part in causing that, if I could take it back, I would in a heartbeat'

'No, it was a different one. My father was there ...' trailing off, I refuse to tell him any more than I already have.

'He cannot harm you, I will not allow it' indicating the guards stationed outside ' you have my best men guarding you twenty four hours a day.'

Standing up straight, as if coming to a decision, he walks towards me 'can I hold you? I just want to feel you next to me, nothing else. You are well within your rights to reject me if you wish, it is nothing more than I deserve.'

I realise that I want nothing more than to be held by this complicated man, who has held me captive, in more ways than one, from the minute I laid eyes on him; nodding slowly I pull back the blankets as he climbs in and lays next to me.

'Oh Mi pequeno pajaro, I have missed you so much' placing small kisses on my eyes, he holds me close; I am amazed at how well out bodies mould together, it is as if we were made for each other.

Falling into a restful sleep; the first one in nearly two weeks, Dalton continues to hold me tight. I have not felt this safe, protected and loved in a long time. With Dalton holding me the nightmares do not return; I sleep peacefully.

When I wake up, Dalton is no longer in the bed with me. I am not sure how long he has been gone, but I miss his touch already. I can hear Sophia cooking in the kitchen, and decide to go and see if I can help her, still unaccustomed to having things done for me.

'Where are you going?' Dalton sticks his head around the bathroom door, with a huge grin on his face; his hair is damp from having a shower. 'Come here, I've run you a bath. When you've finished, I'll rub the ointment on that Pedro has left.'

This man never ceases to surprise me; walking towards him I return his smile. Stepping into the bathroom, he closes the door firmly behind me.

'Can I?' indicating that he would like to help me undress, I lift my arms up, waiting for him to pull the top off of my body. As he gets his first look at the sores covering my frail body the pain he is feeling is evident in his voice, 'fuck Mi pequeno pajaro, look at what I did to you' He continues to carefully remove the rest of my clothing, before lifting me like a child and placing me in the bath. He begins to undress, but seeing my raised eyebrow he stops. 'Can I join you? I just want to take care of you. I promise I won't try anything, unless of course, you want me to' winking he continues to undress, and I get a ringside view of his amazing erection.

I begin to feel the stirrings of lust deep inside of me, oh god, I really want him to try something.

Stepping into the bath; sitting opposite me, he reaches for my foot and begins to massage it; it feels strangely erotic; especially when his hands begin to snake up my leg. He doesn't take his eyes off of my face, gauging my reaction to his touch. The anticipation as his hands head further north, has me holding my breath, waiting for him to touch me where I long to be touched. His hands reach behind my buttocks and pull me towards him; now straddling him, he places small gentle kisses on my partly open mouth. Eagerly kissing him back, he begins to withdraw, and pushes me away slightly. Moving my hands behind his head, I try desperately to reconnect and deepen the contact, he pulls my hands away from him and gently kisses each palm, before placing each finger into his mouth, nibbling on the pad as he pulls it out, the sensation created makes me gasp in delight.

'Mi pequeno pajaro, please, let me love you. I have missed you so much, I am afraid that I will hurt you. Lets take it slow, ok?'

Disappointed at his reluctance for a repeat performance from over a week ago, I nod sadly. I realise that I am desperate to feel him inside of me, to make me his once again.

Pulling me towards him once more, he continues softly kissing me, his lips moving down each side of my neck, I could feel my heart racing, desperate for him to be rough with me. Moving my legs behind him, he places me, between his legs. Reaching behind his back, he begins to gently massage my feet again, slowly moving his hands up my legs, with gentle kneading motions. Desperately trying to move myself towards him, so I could plunge his cock deep inside of me, but holding me firmly in place he looks into my eyes once more, a grin forming at the corner of his mouth as he shakes his head.

'Mi pequeno pajaro, have patience; I want to make love to you, not fuck you. Please just stay still, if you move again I will have to leave'

Nodding at him; but still trying to work out the difference between making love and fucking, knowing that I do not want him to leave me; but that I also desperately want his cock inside of me, to give me the ecstasy that only he can provide, I stay as still as possible.

Seeing my disappointment; he pushes me back, making

me rest against the bath tub; he gently begins easing two fingers inside of me; teasing me with slow, shallow, rhythmic thrusts. His thumb rubbing my clitoris; making me gasp when he increases the pressure, whilst his fingers continue their teasing. I can feel the heat in my core rising, my face becoming flushed. Feeling a slight pressure on my sphincter, I know what is coming next; as his little finger inserts into my anus, I can't help but gasp with the sensation of a mix of pleasure and pain. With the same teasing rhythm, he slowly drives deeper into me. Feeling me tighten, an orgasm ready to take a grip, his thrusting becomes quicker. My orgasm comes in shock waves making my body vibrate with ecstasy. When he is sure that the last of the waves are over, he slows the thrusting and begins to tease me again, it doesn't take long before my core begins to tighten again. Returning his stare as he watches my facial expression as I cum again, screaming his name. As the last of my orgasm ripples away, I rest my head on the lip of the bath as he withdraws his fingers from inside of me.

Waiting to feel his cock dive deep into me, I disappointedly watch him as he stands up in the bath, steps over the side of the tub and beings to dry him self. The intense stare he is giving me is creating my core to quiver in excitement. Lifting me out of the bath he reaches for the towel that is on the hook next to me, my mouth is partly open, waiting for his tongue to take me in a passionate kiss. Wrapping the towel around me he pulls me close, kissing me, before gently patting me dry. The silence is deafening as he begins to apply the ointment to my sore skin. He has barely said a word to me, have I done something wrong?

Picking me up by my waist, he perches me on the counter

of the Jack and Jill sinks. Moving closer to me he tilts my chin towards him, gently kissing me on the mouth. I return his kiss with hungry passion, placing my arms around him, drawing him closer; I can feel his erection between us, I want him so badly. I can feel a change in him as he begins to kiss me back with as much passion as I am kissing him. He removes the towel wrapped around me and before I know what if happening my breast is in his mouth; biting my nipple causing shock waves of ecstasy to ripple through me, settling in my now throbbing core.

Throwing my head back, I hear his name on my lips, my legs wrapping around his waist; eager to feel him inside of me.

My actions have a sobering effect on him, he freezes before letting go of me and wrapping the towel around my shoulders. Walking away from me, he stops in the doorway, looking over his shoulder he says 'I'll leave you to get dressed; Sophia will have dinner ready for you soon.'

And with that he is gone. I am hopeful that he will join me for dinner, but when I enter the dining room, there is only one place setting made up. After years of eating alone, I persuade Sophia to sit and eat with me. The meal was delicious, but I barely manage a few mouthfuls.

My emotions and thoughts are in turmoil at Daltons sudden exit, I excuse myself from the table, and returned to the relative safety of my room. Curling up on my bed, I cry myself to sleep, waiting for the nightmares to return, almost sure that Daltons rejection meant that he would send me away again.

I woke the following morning, surprised that the nightmares didn't surface during the night; feeling a crushing weight across my chest and thighs, I suddenly knew the reason why; turning my head slightly I can see Daltons sleeping form lying next to me with one arm and leg resting heavily over my body, pinning me to the bed. Without feeling his erection in my side, I know that he is in a deep sleep.

    Resisting the temptation to run my finger along his cheek, I lay watching him; waiting for him to wake. Unable to ignore the call of Mother Nature any longer, I carefully move his arm off of my body; the movement seems to disturb him, as he rolls over removing his leg from me, along with most of the sheets. Holding my breath I look at his back whilst carefully putting my feet on the floor, and padding quietly to the bathroom, I hear movement coming from the bed and can feel him watching him. Turning to look at him, I am rewarded with a lazy smile, which makes my heart skip a beat. This is ridiculous, how can someone I barely know have such an effect on me?

    Locking myself in the bathroom, I look at my reflection in the mirror; gone is the haunted look in my eyes, they have been regained the usual sparkle that I am used to seeing. Trying to regain some form of composure, I need time to think; my reaction to his presence is unnerving; I need to find a way to avoid him so my brain can regain control. Maybe then I would be able to formulate a plan to escape; much as the surroundings are beautiful, I do not like the feeling of being held a prisoner. But how can I repel his advances; he only has to look at me and my lust begins to flutter. What if I do manage the impossible; would he send me back to the cabin, and make me service his men? I would rather die than go back to that place. I am going to have to try to take control of the situation; let him do whatever he wants to do to me, and try my hardest not to fall for him. Knowing that this is going to be a very difficult task, I unlock the bathroom door, to face my demons.

Leaving the bathroom, I can feel that he is no longer in the room; and one look at the now empty bed confirms this, I breath a sigh of relief, at least my resolve will not be tested straight away. Deciding on my next course of action whilst getting dressed, I hear Sophia in the kitchen making breakfast; the smell of freshly cooked pancakes makes by stomach grumble. Remembering that I barely ate last night; and seeing as how I am now determined to find a way to escape, I need to keep my strength up, and breakfast seems as good a place to start as anywhere.

Entering the kitchen, I see plates piled high with pastries, pancakes and fresh fruit; my mouth is watering. My stomach begins to complain at the teasing aromas coming from the table.

'Morning Sophia' I sing in greeting.

Startled, she turns with a wary smile on her face, 'morning miss,' her eyes signalling to the corner of the room.

Looking in the direction she indicates; fighting everything I have not to run, I see Marcus standing there with a coffee cup clasped in both of his hands, whilst leaning lazily on the countertop, his feet are crossed at the ankles. Motionless, I stare at him, the last time I saw him he was dragging me away to the Cabin, the memory brought with it the fear from my time there and of the hell that I had endured; my hands begin to get clammy and I can hear my heart beating in my ears as the colour drains from my face.

Sophia seeing me frozen in fear "accidently" drops a plate, the sound of it smashing on the hard tiles, breaks me out of my trance.

Marcus seeming unfazed at my reaction to him drains his coffee, before placing his cup in the sink. Walking towards me, chuckling to him self as I begin to move away from him; my absolute fear of him seems to cause him great amusement, 'Dalton wants to see you. He said to let you eat first, so I'll wait right here for you' pulling up a chair at the table he sits down heavily, smiling widely at me, waiting for what he knows is coming next.

'I'm not hungry' suddenly my appetite was gone; the memory of the last time this monster came to fetch me was still imprinted on my mind. After Daltons rejection of me last night, I am beginning to wonder if he is having second thoughts about having me back at the house. Will I be sent away again?

'Please yourself, let's go' Marcus stands up noisily, scraping the chair across the tiles as he pushes it back underneath the table.

Following behind Marcus I have never felt so scared in all of my life; especially when two of the guards from the apartment bring up the rear. This is it. I am being sent away again. Fearing the worst, my pace begins to slow; looking around desperately for somewhere to run and hide, to get away from what I am sure is about to happen. I am somewhat surprised that I don't feel the expected push in my back from the guards behind, forcing me to pick up the pace; instead they simply slow their pace to match mine.

Looking over his shoulder Marcus sees that we have fallen behind; and stops, waiting patiently for us to catch up. He doesn't seem annoyed, or irritated with me, when I also stop. Is this some new form of torture that I haven't heard about? When is he going to pull me by the hair, to force me to walk quicker, or slap me around the face with anger, and when are the guards going to jab me in the back with their rifle butts. Looking around at them, expecting some form of punishment for stopping, I am surprised when they just nod their heads, waiting for me to move forwards of my own accord.

I quickly look back towards Marcus when I hear his footsteps coming towards me. I must look like a startled rabbit caught in the headlights, as he stops moving, and raises his hands in a calming motion.

'Eloise, no one is going to hurt you, I swear; Dalton just wants to speak with you, that's all. Calm down.'

I am frozen to the spot with fear. Struggling to breath as panic sets in, every breath feels as if I am drowning, gasping for air, trying desperately to stay afloat; failing to give my brain the oxygen it needs, my eyesight begins to blur and my fingers begin to tingle. Someone catches me just before I hit the floor, I can feel them running with me in their arms, shouting Daltons name. Everything begins to go black.

When I come around, I am laying on the sofa in Daltons office. Pedro is kneeling next to me taking my vital signs, when he is satisfied that I am ok he looks at Dalton; who is pacing the room watching me. Pedro begins to speak in Spanish and the relief washes over Daltons face as the tension leaves his body.

Marcus is the first to speak, 'Eloise, I am so, so sorry,' as he leaves the room.

Pedro follows shortly afterwards, leaving me alone with Dalton.

He doesn't move from the spot where he stands rooted, hands in his pockets as if deciding what to say.

My voice sounds like a desperate mouse, 'are you sending me away again?' needing to know, but not sure what his response will be.

'No,' looking relieved that he has made the decision, he continues, 'but we need to talk.'

I manoeuvre myself into a sitting position, waiting to hear what he has to say next. I have so many questions that I want the answers to, but allow him to speak first.

'How much do you remember about the night your parents died?' Dalton is still standing, not able to decide if he should sit next to me.

'Not a great deal; and until recently I couldn't remember anything' I relay to him the memory that had surfaced in my recent nightmare, relief showing on his face when he realised that he wasn't the cause of the one he had witnessed. Hoping that he is able to tell me that I am wrong, and that my mother is also still alive.

Dalton moves to sit on the sofa opposite me, listening intently to my memory of my parents.

'I think Marcus should hear this; he needs to know that he is not the whole reason for your panic attack. The doctor thinks you have a form of PTSD, and Marcus feels as if his actions towards you are responsible' seeing my reticence at having him in the same room as me, he adds, 'Marcus is a good man, he wouldn't intentionally hurt someone. Please allow him to come back into the room so he can explain his actions. When you have heard what he has to say, you can decide if you want him to continue overseeing your security detail.'

The journalist in me is intrigued; eager for more information, I meekly nod my head.

'Marcus, you can come back in now. But move as far away from the door as possible. Ell if you feel the need to leave you can; there are two guards the other side of the door, wherever you go, they go,'

Marcus slowly enters the room, giving me a wide birth as he stands in the far corner of the room, trying not to make any sudden moves.

Watching him suspiciously, waiting for some form of attack, 'am I a prisoner?'

'No,' seeing me look in the direction of the closed door, 'the guards are there for your protection; there have been death threats made against you.'

With a dry mouth, I whisper, 'from whom?' unable to comprehend why someone would want to hurt me.

'Dalton, I think we should concentrate on other things first. We need to get to the bottom of this' Marcus has not moved from his position, he speaks quietly as if worried that another panic attack may set in.

'Ell, Marcus is right. I promise to tell you everything; but first, can you tell Marcus what you just told me about your dream. He needs to understand what just happened'

'I thought you were going to send me away again, I panicked, that's it.' Sighing, I relented, and told Marcus of my dream.

After I'd finished relaying my story, the two men looked at each other, before Dalton gave a quick nod of his head. I'm intrigued as to what unhidden message had passed between them.

'Marcus, bring me the file on my desk please,' Dalton watches my reaction as Marcus moves closer to me; realising that I am about to bolt, he stands and takes the file from Marcus' hand, before sitting next to me.

'This file is a police report from the night your mother was killed' I instantly reach for it, I have to know what happened that night, he places his hand over mine and holds onto it, turning to look at me, 'you can look at it if you like, I won't stop you. But in the meantime I will give you a breakdown of what we know; from this point,' tapping the file, 'to where we are now.'

'After my father confronted yours with the evidence of his sideline, your father went underground. He covered his tracks very well, because despite trying to find him, he didn't resurface until his supposed death 15 years ago. Numerous people informed us that his wife, your mother, left him when she discovered what he had been doing. She was so disgusted by his actions, that she became an informant, and told the police everything that she knew about his business dealings. You were both placed in a witness protection scheme, but your father continued bribing officers until he found you. He murdered your mother as she ran upstairs to protect you from him. We think he planned to take you with him, but a police siren disturbed him. He left a body of a man; similar in age and appearance as him, and paid off the pathologist who was dealing with the case; to make it look like he had died that night as well. What we didn't understand, until recently, is why there is no mention of you? There is no record of your birth, you were never enrolled in any schools, the witness protection documents do not even mention a child, the police officer that was first on the scene makes no mention of you either. It's as if your existence has been wiped away.'

'I don't understand, I went to school; I remember it. Why would someone erase my life?'

'For your protection; your father has a great many enemies who would love to use you to exact revenge on your father.'

I cannot control the shaking that has taken over me, Dalton holds me tight, trying to calm me down, fearful that another panic attack would take me over. Despite his current show of affection towards me, I have to know if he means me harm as well; after all my father is responsible for committing terrible crimes against him and his family, 'Including you?'

'No, never me.' Turning me to look into his eyes, 'admittedly, when I first found out who you were, I wanted to punish you; cut you up into little pieces and send them to your father. But a wise women reminded me "a daughter is not responsible for the sins of her father".'

'Marcella?' Weeping at the realisation that this lady had saved my life more than once, and that I owe her a great debt, one that I can possible never repay.

Nodding, he holds me tight, waiting for the tears to subside.

'Can I ask you something?' before waiting for him to respond, I ask anyway. 'If you are so against trafficking, why are all those women at the Cabin, being forced into prostitution?'

'What? Who told you such a thing? Those women are free to do whatever they please?' Looking at Marcus for an explanation of why I would think such a thing of him.

"Ah,' Marcus looking sheepish begins to explain, 'please understand that I thought she was a plant. I may have implied that the women were prostitutes, and she would have to earn money to pay towards her keep. I can't apologise enough. Ell, the women at the camp have been rescued from operations like your fathers; they are treated by our doctors and offered counselling if required, some of them choose to stay here, knowing that they are safe. Those that wish to make a new life are found homes and jobs on the mainland. Most of the women that live there are married to the men and have started families with them.'

'But Esme, I heard you with her?'

Marcus begins to blush and tells me, 'Esme is my wife.'

'We'll discuss this later Marcus' Dalton is absolutely fuming that Marcus would lead me to believe the worst of him.

'Marcus, I think you are right, I think I am a plant, although not realising it. You say that you've received two notes; one around the same time as I received my tip off, and the second one after I had arrived here? If my father is the man you say he is, I believe that he is using me to get the backing to start a war against you.'

'Dalton, it is plausible. He would do anything to get back at your family; he blames you for his misfortune, he lost virtually everything when your father confronted him.'

'One other thing, the death threats made against me, who are they from?'

'Virtually every crime family in the world wishes to harm you in some way, even those that are aligned with and loyal to me. The ones that are not loyal to me want to use you to hurt me, the rest want to use you to hurt your father in some way. Although I very much doubt that it would hurt him as much as it would hurt me.'

How can my life be turned on its head like this? In less than a month my life has changed so dramatically; from being an undercover journalist, to a woman who is wanted by most of the worlds crime families to exact revenge on two people, one of whom I didn't even realise existed a few short weeks ago. Anger begins to boil inside of me; for the life I should still be living, and anger for the girl long forgotten.

'This is both of your faults. Between you, you have destroyed my entire life; you abducted me, held me prisoner, and made me fear for my life, and now crime cartels want to use me to hurt others.'

Marcus looks at me apologetically, admittedly everything he has done to me was done to protect Dalton, but I cannot forgive him for the lasting damage that he has inflicted on me. I am feeling slightly pleased that he feels somewhat responsible for the danger that he took part in placing me in. Dalton, however, refuses to look at me, he is already aware of the responsibility he shares for the anger that I am now in.

'Dalton, you need to tell her, I still think it's crazy and she won't agree, but she needs to be told'

I look towards Dalton, hoping for some form of an apology, and confirmation that he has decided to set me free. He must know people that can provide me with fake documents so that I can start a new life, far away from him and the danger that he has brought into it. The next words that come out of his mouth make it clear that he has no intention of letting me go anywhere.

'Ell, we, or rather I, have come up with a plan to protect you, and to keep you safe forever. The guards, whilst they are loyal to me at the moment, can be bought. We already know that we have at least one spy living here; and given time we will find out who that person is. But, I feel the best way to protect you is to make you my wife.'

'No,' standing I move towards the door, desperate to be away from these men and their ludicrous plan. What is he talking about; I can't marry him. Of all the absurd ideas, this has to take the biscuit. 'I can't marry you; you're supposed to love, honour and cherish the person that you marry, you make a commitment to them. Marriage is not something that can be turned into a business arrangement that is formed out of some sense of guilt.' With that I leave them, my guards that quickly step into pace behind me, make me even more upset. I feel hot tears running down my cheeks as I make my way back to the apartment that is now my new prison; despite being assured that I am not a prisoner, I can't help but feel like one.

Locking myself in my apartment, I sit on one of armchairs looking out at the stunning view; the gorgeous blue of the ocean and the sounds of the waves crashing upon the shore are lost on me. I sit staring, churning over the details from the last few hours. Marry him? Absolutely ridiculous; there has to be another way out of this situation. The women that he has rescued from enslavement were able to have normal lives after the horrors they were subjected to; this is what I want. I want to be able to have a normal life; and one day be able to marry a man that I love and have his children; and for those children not to live in fear of retribution because of who their father is, or what their father has done to others. But above all else, I want to be free.

Sometime later there is a gentle knock at the apartment door, lost in my thoughts I automatically assume that I would find Sophias friendly face on the other side. Opening the door with a smile, which quickly fades as I see Dalton standing there. I place my foot behind the door, using it as a security blanket; at least if he tries to barge his way in, my foot will make it slightly harder for him to gain access. I stand quietly looking at him, waiting for him to speak; I have nothing else to say to him.

'May I come in? I had to see you, to check if you were

ok' Dalton looks pained as I weigh up my options; before opening the door wider and moving away from him. 'I feel I need to explain some things to you; these threats are real, people want to hurt you. I'm sorry if you felt that my marriage proposal was a business arrangement; it isn't, I just want to keep you safe. As my wife, the only people that will try to hurt you are those loyal to your father. It greatly diminishes the threat towards you; as there are only a few people loyal to you father. I also feel somewhat responsible for putting you in danger.'

'Good I am glad that you feel responsible because you are. I can't marry you; there is no love between us. We would end up hating each other, I'd rather die than live a life like that' turning away from him, seeing the pain in his eyes from my outburst I move towards the patio doors, I need to make as much space between us as possible, before he sees my heart breaking. As I reach for the handle to open the doors, I feel him behind me, placing his hand against the doors, stopping them from opening.

'We don't need love, when we have this' I can feel his erection on the curve of my back, bending down he begins nibbling on the sensitive part of my neck, suddenly biting down hard and making me gasp. I reach behind me, grabbing handfuls of his hair, tilting my head towards him, eager for deeper contact. Unable to understand how he has this effect on me and why I am unable to resist him, my body craves his touch, betraying me every time he is near.

Turning me in his arms he bends down and picks me up, carrying me to my bedroom, and kicking the door closed behind us. Looking down at me, his eyes so full of lust as he carefully places me on the bed, 'I could never get tired of looking at you; you are so beautiful.'

I am quivering inside, excitement building, waiting for what I know is going to happen next, eager to feel him inside of me again.

He begins to slowly undress me, kissing each bit of flesh that is gradually exposed; the sensation has my senses in overdrive.

As each nipple becomes visible through the sheer fabric of my bra, he teases them with his tongue; urging them into soft peaks. Ripping my bra off of me, eager to take an erect nipple into his mouth, swirling his tongue around the tender bud. Alternating between soft teasing licks and hard bites, my breath comes in ragged drags, feeling the wetness between my legs, waiting for him to claim me.

With each hand holding my breasts; teasing my nipples, pinching with nail and finger pad, he begins to trail soft kisses further south, following the line on my abdomen from breast to naval. Holding my breath in anticipation as he removes my pants, placing my knees on his shoulders he plunges his head between my legs. My hands are instantly in his hair; pulling him closer as he sucks on my clitoris and labia, he slowly inserts one finger into the soft folds of flesh between my legs, gently thrusting in long, slow strokes, continuing the assault of his tongue on the sensitive cluster of nerves. I feel my core begin to tighten, an orgasm ready to explode. My nerve endings are on fire, relishing the sweet release of pleasure I know is soon to come; but just as I begin to feel the waves crash over me, he stops. A moan of disappointed escapes my lips; I begin to gyrate my hips, eager for him to continue his assault upon me.

Looking up at me, smiling, he says, 'Marry me'

'No'

I am unable to say anything else as he begins to lick my now very sensitive clitoris, making me gasp. He inserts two fingers, just as slowly as previously and begins teasing me all over again. I can feel my orgasm building, as my core tightens, my body pleading for the release that an orgasm will give it. Just as I am about to scream his name in ecstasy; he stops again, leaving me confused, and on the brink of a powerful orgasm that would tip me over the abyss. I watch as he stands, teasingly removing his clothes as he looks into my eyes, the lust clearly evident in them. Removing his trousers, my gaze travels to his engorged cock, evidence of his arousal. I could never get tired of looking at him naked.

Lying on the bed next to me, he begins to play with the peaks of my nipples, making them even more erect under his touch. Pinching one with the pad of a finger and his thumbnail, the pain and pleasure causing me to arch my back, willing for him enter me again. Closing his mouth around an erect bud, he begins sucking hard, his hand searching for the soft mound of nerve endings between my legs, slowly entering me with four fingers; the feeling of being stretched has me on the precipice of a fast approaching orgasm. Begging silently that he will finally let me cum, my body vibrating with pleasure, getting closer and closer to jumping over the edge.

His hand becomes still inside of me, his assault on my nipple stops as he pulls away, blowing cold air on the sensitive peak.

Looking pleadingly into my eyes 'Marry me'
'No'
His lips are on my mouth crushing them in a passionate kiss, his tongue seeking entry; which is soon granted. I moan as

his hand begins to twist slowly inside of me, stretching me even more than I thought was possible Slowly pulling out, then just as slowly pushing inside of me, twisting and then pulling out again.

Looking down at me, he continues his slow teasing, watching my face as an orgasm begins to rise.

Again, just as I am about to explode in ecstasy, he stops, 'marry me'

Now understanding his game of trying to fuck me into submission, I smile up at him, 'no'

He thrusts his fingers and thumb deep inside of me, making me gasp in shock and pleasure. Claiming my mouth once more whilst he thrusts harder, quickening his pace; bringing me to the point of climax, as he changes rhythm my orgasm fades away.

He continues this assault several times; each time bringing me to the point of climaxing before stopping, asking me to marry him, and then starting all over again.

Unable to continue with the torturous teasing of both of us, he moves above me; placing himself between my open legs, he rests his cock at the entrance to my vagina, I am holding my breath in anticipation; waiting for him to slam into me; to give me what I so desperately need.

Looking down at me, smiling, he asks 'Could you live your life like this?' before slamming into me.

One thrust was enough to make waves of orgasm wash over me. His pace was relentless, pushing though my tightening folds. The constant thrusting causing me to be pushed up the bed; slipping his arms underneath my body he holds my shoulders tight, stopping all movement. Pulling me down onto each thrust, deepening the thrusts of his invading cock into me.

With sweat pooling in the valley between my breasts, he shows no signs of tiring, slamming his cock so deep into me that I can feel him hit the roof of my vagina, the pain that it causes is quickly forgotten as another orgasm is fast approaching.

All of a sudden he pulls out of me, standing, he walks to the other side of the room, making as much distance between us as possible, 'Well could you?'

Confusion hits; I'm still in the heady space of ecstasy, my lungs gasping for breath, my brain craving oxygen to clear the fog caused by his relentless teasing.

'Could I what?' my voice comes out of my mouth breathlessly, as I try to get my breathing back under control.

Watching the wicked glint in his eyes, as he knows that I am ready to cave and give in to him. 'Could you live your life like this? My cock buried deep inside of you, giving you what no other man can.'

'Yes, I think I could.'

'Then marry me. Not just for your protection, but also for mine. I wouldn't survive if anything was to happen to you.' looking at me, straight into my eyes, the look of lust replaced by something else.

'We can't get married, we don't even know each other.'

Pacing towards me, like a panther stalks its prey, he continues to stare at me, his eyes following the curves of my body. 'All I know is how your body responds to my touch, and how mine responds to yours. I know how you feel when I bury myself deep inside of you. I know how you feel when you begin to tighten around my cock milking it until I cum alongside you. I know that I will never get bored of looking at you, or fucking you; I'd go to war for you. Isn't that enough for now?'

His hands are tracing the line on my abdomen from breast to navel, small slow strokes, my nerves are on fire again; I cannot think straight when he is touching me. I try to move away from his touch, before I say, or do, something I may regret later. Grabbing hold of my legs, he places them over his shoulders as he drives his cock deep inside of me, I scream in pleasure at the unexpected invasion. He begins to make slow deep thrusts; making me feel all that he has to give. As I relax and open up to him fully, he is hitting my roof, before withdrawing completely. Each time he withdraws my body craves for him to be inside of me again; I could hear soft moans of longing leave my lips each time. The pain from having him balls deep inside of me has gone, now all I can feel is complete pleasure, lost in the moment with him.

Slipping his hands underneath my shoulders he picks me up; worried that he may drop me, I wrap my arms around his neck for purchase, as he continues to thrust slowly into me. The angle of his cock entering me hits all the right spots; I feel my core begin to tighten as an orgasm is fast approaching. Placing my back against the wall, grasping my waist, he begins to pound his cock into me, my back hitting the wall with each thrust. I can feel the weight of his balls as they hit my behind. He leans down and begins biting the hollow of my neck; the sensation that this creates is so powerful, that I can barely breath. He still continues his relentless pounding; my body going into spasms as each orgasm rides on the back of the previous one. Trailing kisses and nibbles up my neck before claiming my mouth in a passionate kiss, I feel him start to swell inside of me; hot semen spurting into me as he screams my name.

'Elly, marry me, please' looking into my eyes, I see a

spark of fire ignite, an unspoken promise that he will always take care of me.

I begin to weigh up my options; Dalton does not appear the sort of man to accept rejection easily. If I continue to refuse, he will simply up the stakes in his sexual torture routine. I can either submit to a life ruled by his sexual deviances; I have no doubt that despite insisting he doesn't wish to hurt me, there is a world of depravity lurking beneath the surface. Or, I can agree to marry him. Surely if the threats against me have been overcome, the security detail around me will be relaxed slightly, giving me a means to escape.

'Yes' is all that I can manage as he claims my mouth in a victorious kiss.

SIX

Waking the next morning the house is a hive of activity; I can hear Magda giving people her orders, following her voice, curious as to the cause of all of the commotion, I find her standing in the middle of the huge entrance hall with Dalton by her side.

Dalton senses my presence before Magda notices my arrival; looking up smiling, he begins to saunter towards me, the look that he gives me makes my heart miss a beat. In another lifetime that man could easily be a male model, women would flock to him just to spend time in his presence. Picturing women clamouring for his attention caused a pang of jealousy to shoot through me.

I need to start trying to get a grip of my reaction to him; if I don't, leaving him will become nigh on impossible. I am still forever hopeful that after this shame of a marriage has taken place the security measures around me will be relaxed, giving me the opportunity for escape. At the moment, wherever I go there is always at least two guards following my every move, admittedly they are very respectful and they keep their distance, but I still know that they are there. The only privacy I have is in the confines of my apartment. Having lived on my own for so long, I am unaccustomed to having so many people around me twenty-four hours a day. I respect that their primary role is to keep me safe, but I still yearn for the freedom of being able to go where I please without an armed escort.

Dalton slips his arms around my waist and pulls me in for a tender kiss, 'Magda is beside herself with excitement. She has already begun to plan our wedding, if you have any thoughts or ideas I would tell her now before she gets too carried away.'

Looking at Magda holding her clipboard, giving a small army of people their instructions, she looks so happy, and totally engrossed in organising the wedding, that I am already having second thoughts about.

'No, it's fine.'

Suspecting that I may be having second thoughts about agreeing to his ludicrous marriage proposal, he pulls me to one side, indicating to the guards to keep their distance, 'Is everything ok? You don't seem as excited about our upcoming wedding as I would imagine a bride should be.'

Wondering if I should tell him that I have actually changed my mind, and if he can drop me off on the mainland, that'd be great. He can rest easy knowing that I am out of his hair and that he is no longer responsible for me. However, one look at the darkness entering his eyes tell me that it would be a big mistake.

'I'm fine, just a little tired. I wasn't expecting the plans to be taking shape so soon. I thought it would be nice to have a long engagement, you know, to get to know each other a little bit better.'

'No, we are getting married in three days time. People have already been notified, and will begin to arrive tomorrow morning. The flowers and catering are being organised, and tailors will be flown in tomorrow morning to begin making your gown. Padre Marcelous will marry us at the Island chapel, where my parents were married and I was christened. He will meet us for dinner this evening. Everything is being taken care of.'

'Wow, that's quick. Your doing, or Magdas?' I am in shock; I at least thought that I would have had time to persuade him to rethink his plan. Three days does not give me much time to formulate a plan.

Holding me around the back of my neck, he pulls me close, the anger that is flowing from his pores is frightening. 'Do I need to remind you of the threats that have been made?' forcing me to look up at him, making sure that his words sink in, 'the quicker we get married, the quicker the threats diminish. This is for your own good.'

Seeing the fear in my eyes, he releases me and takes a step back. He has the ability to heighten my emotions, be they lust or fear, I have to try to regain some control of my life, or I will be nothing but a puppet on his string.

'I … err … I thought that I may go for a walk' nearly adding, "If that's ok" but then deciding that I really don't need his permission.

'Where would you like to walk?' snapping his fingers at the guards to get their attention, they are moving towards us as I answer.

'I spotted a little cove from the balcony of my old room, I thought it would be nice to go for a swim' the thought of standing in the warm ocean with the waves crashing over me fills me with happiness. Although I had spent years living in the city, the thing I missed most about my childhood was the feeling of the ocean moving around your legs as the waves hit the shoreline. I could already taste the saltiness of the seawater in my mouth.

Holding his hand up towards the guards, they stop moving towards us and stand to attention some distance away. 'No, it isn't safe. If you want to swim, I suggest you make use of the private pool your quarters offer you.' With his mind made up, he looked towards the guards, 'Take Eloise back to her apartment and double the guards around her.' Glancing over at me, taking in my anger at being denied a reasonable request. 'Sorry Eloise, but I don't trust you enough to believe that you would not go against my wishes.'

'This is ridiculous, I am a grown women, and you can't keep me a prisoner here indefinitely.' Trying to control my anger, whilst avoiding making a spectacle of myself, and throwing my rattle out of the proverbial pram, I stomp back towards my apartment, before Dalton can say any more.

A feeling of glee escapes me as I slam the door in the faces of the guards that follow too close behind me. Petty I know, but I couldn't help myself. As I enter the sitting room I see that Daltons guards work quickly; the guard detail has indeed been doubled. Whereas previously, the guards were only stationed outside of the doors, they were now inside of the apartment as well; I had to weave between them to access my room; there were even guards stationed at my bedroom door. With my hand on the handle, I prayed that I would at least be afforded some privacy in the sanctuary of my room. Holding my breath I open the door, looking cautiously around, I let out a sigh of relief, thankful that there were no guards in my room. But the detail on the doors outside has been doubled, as well as around the pool area.

Determined not to become a martyr and sit and sulk, I

decided that I might as well make use of the pool. It was stiflingly hot outside, so a dip in the cool water of the pool would do me some good. Stripping off my clothes, I walk into the dressing room. Rifling through the draws, I select a small strappy bikini, it reminded me of the old song "itsy bitsy teeny weeny yellow polka dot bikini" except that it was cerise pink. Yes, this would do, if the guards wanted to watch me, I'd give them something to look at. I couldn't help feeling a little smug; knowing that Dalton would not appreciate the guards staring at me in this. Before nerves could get the best of me, and I could change my mind; I reach for a pair of sunglasses, a kimono wrap and a magazine, planning on spending the day by the pool, sunbathing and swimming.

Leaving my room, the guards fall into step behind me, as I walk down the hallway towards the doors that would take me to the rear patio and pool area. I lengthen my stride, making my hips sway even more as I walk, a small smile on my lips; hoping that they are enjoying the show behind me.

The heat of the midday sun hit me as soon as I stepped outside, the water of the pool looks so inviting that I dive straight into it, the cooling water having the desired effect. Breaking the surface of the water, I take a large lungful of air before sinking beneath the surface and swimming to the opposite end of the pool. Lifting myself out, and walking to the wooden loungers, I notice that my bikini top has slipped exposing a soft pink nipple, adjusting it back into place as I walk; although I wanted to give the guards a show, exposing myself wasn't on my list of priorities. Settling onto the lounger and closing my eyes, I drifted into a peaceful sleep.

Sophia disturbs me sometime later; apparently our dinner

guest has arrived early, and has decided to introduce himself to me without Dalton being present. Feeling somewhat embarrassed by my choice of swimwear as the Padre approaches me, Sophia, ever attentive, passes the kimono to me, which I take from her gratefully before standing to put it on.

Extending my hand to him in greeting as he approaches me, 'Padre Marcelous, it's lovely to meet you'

With a chuckle and a warm smile that reaches his eyes, he sits on the lounger opposite me, indicating that I should be seated, 'please, sit with me a while' reaching for my hand and placing it on his lap, he enveloped it with his other hand, his fingers placed around my wrist feeling for my pulse. 'My child, I was not always a man of the cloth, I have seen a fair few naked women in my time. I can see why Dalton has chosen to marry you above all of the others.'

I did not like the way he was holding my hand and wrist so firmly, but knew that trying to extricate myself from his grasp could cause a scene. I also didn't like the way he made me feel naked, despite being clothed; the term slime ball comes to mind. I actually find myself hoping that news of his arrival would reach Dalton soon, and he would rescue me from this lecherous old man.

'So, tell me, how did you meet Dalton?' his fingers didn't move from my pulse, applying a small amount of pressure so he could feel the slightest fluctuation in my heart rate.

'I met him at work' it wasn't a lie; I did initially meet him at work.

'I see, and where were you working?'

'I was a waitress at Bar 21' deliberately missing out the part about being an undercover journalist.

Staring at my chest, which made me feel repulsed, 'Isn't that a club for gentlemen, where they are served their orders by topless waitresses?'

My heart begins to beat rapidly, as the memory of how far I was willing to sink to get the story, surfaced, trying desperately to regulate the rhythm before he notices, 'Yes it is, have you been there before?'

A small smile forms on his lips, telling me that he has picked up on the changing rhythm, whether he suspected that I had been caught out in a lie, or if I was simply embarrassed about my chosen career path, he doesn't say, deciding instead to change tact completely. 'And how did he propose? Was it a romantic gesture.'

'I suppose some may call it that.' Would I call it romantic? Definitely not, but I am aware that even the slightest change in my heart rate could cause problems for me. I did not want to anger Dalton; there is no telling what the repercussions would be.

'How long have you known Dalton?'

'A few weeks'

'Are you aware of how wealthy and respected the Mercedes family are?'

'Not really, no; I have no interest in material things.' This wasn't a lie, I had always assumed that having lots of money and not a care in the world was what I aspired to; but now it is being offered to me, I couldn't think of anything I wanted less.

'I do not quite believe you; you say that you have only known him for a few weeks, yet here you are, living in his late mothers apartment, with a wedding to one of the wealthiest bachelors this side of the globe due to take place in a few days, but you say you have no interest in material things. You were a waitress in a seedy bar, you come from nothing, and now you are about to become a very wealthy woman, a real Cinderella story of rags to riches. I need to make you aware that I will be suggesting to Dalton that he has a prenuptial agreement drawn up, I suggest you agree and sign it.'

Deciding that I really don't like this man, or the tone of his implications; I pull my hand away from his, standing, I walk away and tell him over my shoulder, 'Ok, you do that.'

'My child, I have not finished speaking with you, please come and sit with me' the change in his tone should have offered me a warning, but I was so angry I ignored it.

'Well, I'm finished talking to you. Good-bye' I had almost reached the doors leading back into the apartment when I sensed that he was close. The thought "oh shit" came very quickly, as he turned the corner leading to my apartment. The look on his face tells me that he believes that he has seen enough to decide that I am entirely in the wrong, and have behaved extremely rudely.

'Eloise! He is our guest, and you will treat him as such. Go inside, I will speak with you later.'

Turning to look at him as the heat of embarrassment rises in my face; he looks so angry, I could see his body vibrating as he tries to control himself. Walking towards me, I quickly duck inside the cool interior of the apartment, feeling like a naughty child hiding from an angry parent. Closing the door firmly behind me, I watch as the two men greet each other with a firm hug and a gentle slap on the back. They appear to be very good friends, but I suppose if he has been the religious authority in his life, they would be.

Passing the kitchen as I walk to my room, I see Sophia talking quietly into her mobile phone again. Knocking gently on the door to indicate my presence, not wishing to startle her. She panics as she looks up at me, then relief washes over her features, ending her call quickly as I entered the room.

'You ok miss?' Sophia begins to look cautiously around her, wondering if Dalton is hot on my heels.

'Not really, do we have any wine?' If I am going to be forced to spend the evening with that man, I will do so in a drunken protest.

Sophia begins to open the cupboards before finding a bottle of Merlot. Pouring me a small glass, Sophia hands it to me.

'Perfect, thank you' I down the contents in a large gulp. Watching Sophias face as I refill my glass; it is clear that Dalton has told her that I cannot handle alcohol. Taking the glass and the rest of the open bottle, before she can stop me, I retire to my room, content to drown my sorrows for the rest of the afternoon.

After I drain my glass for the third time, Dalton enters my room, his face like thunder. The anger emanating from him

'Explain yourself. Explain why you were so rude to my father.'

'What do you mean "your father?" That man is your father? Then why did he make me believe that he was Padre Marcelous, I even greeted him as such and he didn't once correct me.'

Apparently, he found this funny as I could feel his anger begin to dissipate, 'whether you thought he was the Padre or not; it does not excuse your rudeness towards him.'

'He was rude to me first,' I declare, feeling like a petulant child, 'he as much as called me a liar and a gold digger. I felt as if I were on a lie detector machine whilst he was holding my wrists asking his questions.'

'Ah, my father is a complicated man; loosing my mother changed him. He is just trying to protect his only child; you cannot really blame him.'

The thought of what my father did to his mother leaves me wondering how much his father knows about me 'does he know who my father is, he thinks I'm a gold digger, and at the moment I am not sure what is worse, a gold digger or the daughter of the man that kidnapped and murdered his wife.'

'My father will be joining us for dinner tonight, we can tell him together; he needs to be made aware of who you are, and why we have to get married.'

'Fine, just let me know when the prenup is ready to be signed.'

'Prenup? There will be no prenup; after all you can never leave me, where would you go?' Allowing his words to sink in, he left me with the turmoil of my thoughts.

He was right, where would I go? Everyone who ever cared about me thought I was dead.

The rest of the afternoon drags, and I can't help but feel completely trapped. He is right, I have nowhere to go, my life was destroyed the second he walked into it, and he continues to rule over me, my body betraying me each time he is close.

'Elly.'

Jumping at the sudden interruption, I look up and see Sophia sitting in the chair opposite me.

'Where were you? I've been calling you for ages. It's time to get ready for dinner; and your guests have started to arrive. Senor will be cross if you are late and keep them waiting.'

'Oh, sorry, I must have zoned out for a minute,' looking across at the ocean I could see that the sun had already begun to set; I must have zoned out for longer than I thought. The cool evening breeze, causing the curtains to billow, and goose bumps were forming on my bare skin. Realising that I am still wearing my bikini from earlier, I really need to have a shower before getting ready for dinner and time was running out fast. Not wishing to anger Dalton further I ask Sophia meekly, 'would you mind finding something suitable for me to wear whilst I have a shower? I still smell of chlorine from the pool earlier.'

'Of course, I'll look now for you and lay it out on the bed.'

'Thanks.' Entering the en-suite, I change the shower temperature to the hottest it will allow, turning the water on I begin to strip out of my bikini. Stepping underneath the flowing water, the temperature of the water making my skin turn red on contact, I lather up the shampoo and begin to wash my hair. The smell from the suds reminded me of home, all of a sudden I feel extremely home sick and I begin to sob. My old life seems like a distant memory now, I wish I could turn back time and ignore the lead that was left on my door mat; I would have been quite happy writing teaser pieces for the rest of my life.

Hearing the bathroom door open, I quickly wipe my eyes, hoping that whomever has entered would not realise that I have been having a one-person pity-party in the shower. Quickly rinsing the suds from my hair, I turn off the shower and reach for a towel, wrapping it around myself before turning to look at the person that had entered the bathroom. Dalton is standing with his back leaning against the door, blocking my exit and carefully watching my every move; if he had noticed my tears he didn't mention them. I found it unusual that my spidey-sense didn't pick up on his presence, but I suppose wallowing in self-pity, can have that effect. Taking in his attire of black dress suit, white shirt with a starched collar and a pale blue satin tie, he looked so hot and sexy, making my heart skip a beat. A small part of me couldn't quite believe that he was mine; then I reminded myself that he is not mine, I am his; his prisoner, his sex slave and soon to be his wife, whether I wanted to be or not.

Dalton is still standing by the door, blocking my path, watching me, as if assessing how best to deal with me. I find myself silently praying that he had changed his mind, and that the wedding was cancelled, that he would give me a new identity and set me free.

'We need to talk about this evening' walking towards me in swift strides, stopping abruptly when he was close enough to feel the sparks between our bodies, he reaches out and holds my face forcing me to look into his eyes, making sure that I take in every word he says, 'it is very important that Padre Marcelous believes that after a whirlwind romance, we are very much in love and cannot wait to become man and wife. I cannot stress to you enough how important it is that you play this role well; do you understand? After the Padre has left we will discuss our predicament with my father.'

So the wedding is still going a head, unless the Padre doesn't believe out story of being head over heels in love, or after telling his father another plan is formulated. Praying for a miracle, I nod that I have understood the role that I am being forced to play.

'After seeing how well you played your role at my club, I have no doubt that this will be second nature to you; so if the

Padre doesn't believe it, I will know who to blame.'

Embarrassment floods my cheeks at the memory of my scantily clad "audition", parading around the stage in an almost see through outfit, which left little or nothing to the imagination. Vibrating against a pole, doing my utmost to wear a face that said, "I belong on this stage" all the while wanting to die inside.

As he releases me I push past him, eager to make some space between us to gather my thoughts. On the bed I see that Sophia has laid out a blue satin cocktail dress that would hug all of my curves in all the right places; feeling slightly betrayed that she has chosen the exact same colour of Daltons tie, which will give people the false illusion that we are a happy couple; we are anything but a happy couple.

Keeping my back to him and ignoring the fact that Dalton is still continuing to watch me from the bathroom door, I begin to get dressed. The gown that Sophia has chosen is beautiful; a soft shade of pale blue, strapless with a sweetheart neckline that doesn't show too much cleavage, and fits my small frame perfectly. Drying my hair and putting it up into a messy chignon, I hastily apply some mascara and lip-gloss.

Looking at my now haunted reflection I put on my game face, turning to Dalton saying, 'right, let's get this over with.'

Dalton appears pleased with my appearance, as a small smile plays at his lips, 'You've forgotten something.'

Misunderstanding him, I look at my reflection again, scrutinising my appearance I cannot see anything missing. I feel the heat emanating from Daltons body, as he stands close behind me; he places his hands on my shoulders, running them down my arms and slipping them around my waist, holding my hands that I had instinctively placed there when he began touching me. As he nuzzles into my neck, deeply breathing in my scent, I can see, in the mirror, how his proximity changes my appearance; the heat of my arousal gives my skin a warm glow, my eyes become hooded waiting for an orgasm to rock my body and my mouth is slightly parted as if waiting to be claimed; the haunted look has left my face, to be replaced by the look of lust and wanting. Feeling Dalton slip something onto my ring finger, I look down at my hand. The engagement ring he places there is divine; a large blue gemstone surrounded with smaller black gems, the ring which takes up the whole width of my finger must have cost a small fortune. I cannot accept this; it is too extravagant, and I try to remove it, Dalton places his hands over mine.

'Eloise, please stop.'

'I cannot take this, it's too much. A smaller, simpler ring would have sufficed; the size of this bauble is ridiculous.'

'You are about to become the wife of Dalton Mercedes, you are expected to show signs of our wealth.'

Fabulous, so now I am going to be dressed like a Christmas tree as well. I want to hold my ground, at least try to make him see sense of how ridiculous this all is, but I am also aware that I still have to suffer dinner with three men, two of whom I really don't like very much. Taking a deep breath, I remove myself from Daltons grasp and head towards the front door of the apartment. Walking through the small lounge I see his father is waiting there, seated on one of the chairs overlooking the view, a large glass of amber liquid in his hand. Swilling the liquid absentmindedly, around the glass, before taking a mouthful. Hearing the sound of my heels on the marble floor, he looks up with tears in his eyes, taking a second to compose himself, he smiles as he sees me standing in the room, like a rabbit caught in the headlights.

'Eloise, you look lovely. Please come and sit with me.'

'But Padre Marcelous will be waiting for us.'

'Oh let the old man wait, sit with me; I wanted to apologise to you for earlier. I should have told you who I really was, but I couldn't resist, I am sorry. I find that when people know who I am they are less likely to answer my questions honestly, for fear of reprisals. When I realised that you thought I was the Padre, I decided to play along and get to the bottom of why my son has chosen to marry you. From what I can tell you have no money, or family ties with one of our allies that could strengthen their bond to us, forgive me for being curious' taking another sip from his glass, he turns his head to look at the view.' Daltons mother loved it here you know, she would spend hours with him at the little cove just over there,' pointing at the cove I'd requested to visit earlier, 'she never got to see her apartment finished before she was taken, I'm glad Dalton decided to finish it for her. I think she would have approved, and I think she would have liked you as well.'

Hearing Daltons father reminisce about his wife, knowing that my father was responsible for her death, I could feel a lump forming in my throat. Regaining my composure, I returned meekly, 'thank you.'

'Mi pequeno pajaro, shall we?'

I hadn't even heard Dalton approaching, but here he was standing next to me, offering his arm in an act of chivalry. For the sole purpose of maintaining appearances, I stood and took his arm. Thinking "in for a penny, in for a pound" I tiptoed and placed a small kiss on his lips. The surprise of me instigating affection in front of his father has the desired effect of making him blush.

Daltons father finds this highly amusing, laughing as he says, 'come on love birds, we'd better not keep the Padre waiting any longer.'

As we walk towards the dining room, my stomach grumbles in appreciation at the delicious smell of the food Magda has prepared for us; she is an exceptionally talented chef. The table is set in a formal layout, rather than the buffet that Dalton and I had previously shared in this room. The dinner service is a fine bone china, in white with a thin red line on the outer edge, in stark contrast to the black table. Blood red napkins are folded ornamentally at each place setting, and it seems a shame to unfold and use them. In each corner of the room stands a waiter; each of them dressed immaculately in a white tuxedo, and holding a silver tray at shoulder height with a solitary champagne flute resting on top.

As we approach the table, I see an older gentleman already seated on one side. He appears to be in his late seventies, with grey thinning hair, a definite bald spot just visible beneath the hair he had chosen to comb over to hide it. His face is heavily lined, partly due to age and, judging by his evident tan, partly due to sun worshipping.

'Padre Marcellous thank you for joining us this evening. Apologies for keeping you waiting.' Daltons father greets him with an outstretched hand, which is taken in a firm handshake as the Padre rises to greet us.

'Not a problem at all, I wouldn't miss the opportunity to meet the young lady who has managed to snap up your son. She must be quite something, to manage to get Dalton agree to marriage so quickly into their relationship.'

Hearing the Padres thoughts of me, makes me feel quite uncomfortable. In a civilised society we do not speak about people in their presence, it's just rude.

'Padre, allow me to introduce you to my fiancé; Eloise Mansell'

I politely greet him as his lecherous gaze travels my entire body, I thought that I felt uncomfortable before, but now I feel completely naked under his scrutinising stare.

Dalton guides me to one of the place settings to break the Padres intense scrutiny of me, and pulls the out chair for me to be seated opposite his father and the Padre. With a click of his fingers, the waiters approach the table and deposit the glasses of champagne they are carrying in front of us and each of our guests

Daltons father, tapping his knife against the side of the cut lead crystal champagne flute, and rises from his seat, raising his glass, 'A toast to my son and his beautiful fiancé; proof that true love does exist, and given the short space of time that they have know each other, that time has no meaning. To Dalton and Eloise'

This evening was going from bad to worse, if his father believed that we were in love, how would he feel when he later found out that this marriage was a sham, born out of a sense of duty, and nothing but one of convenience. He still clearly thinks that I am a gold digger, and am simply marrying his son for his money, but the truth is far worse.

Despite spending most of the day dreading this evening, it went particularly well. Daltons father regaled tales of Daltons mischievous childhood antics, which Padre Marcellous took great delight in adding to. I soon got the impression that Padre Marcellous was more than the Island priest; he was also a very close family friend.

The effect of consuming too much food and alcohol had me trying to stifle a yawn towards the end of the evening.

Padre Marcellous doesn't miss a trick and notices how tired I am becoming, 'well Ricardo and Dalton, I must say my farewells. I have eaten more than my fair share of food, and consumed far too much of your delicious wine; which has gone straight to my head. Eloise, it has been an absolute pleasure meeting you. You youngsters make a lovely couple and I am sure that you will make Dalton very happy indeed.'

Rising from our chairs in unison as the Padre leaves the room, Dalton glances down at me before saying, 'Father, we need to talk. Pour yourself a brandy, you are going to need it.'

I could feel the colour draining from my face, the laughter and enjoyment of the evening quickly forgotten, as the moment I had been dreading most of all was finally here. Taking my hand in his, for moral support, Dalton led the way to his office, his father, somewhat bewildered by the change in atmosphere, following closely behind.

Making our way to Daltons office, two of my guards brought up the rear with Marcus following closely behind them. Entering the office, Marcus closes the door firmly behind him, standing with his back against the door, with my two guards remaining in the outer office. There were guards placed outside each window and door, with their backs to the room. I could see the light from inside the room reflecting off of the ear-pieces they wore, and occasionally the light would give the impression of the outline of a gun in the hand of each of the guards. If Daltons father noticed the added security detail, he certainly didn't mention it.

Dalton indicates to his father to sit on one of the sofas, whilst indicating that I sit in the one opposite, Dalton choses to sit next to me, he was so close that he may as well have been sat on my lap; I was unsure if his close proximity to me, was for my benefit or for his.

Taking my hand in his, he cleared his throat before beginning to speak, 'I must warn you, that you will not like this, but please do not interrupt, it is very important that you listen to everything that I have to say.'

Daltons father sits back on the sofa, looking at me suspiciously, correctly assuming that I am the cause of this meeting, with one leg crossed over the other and the glass of brandy firmly clasped in his grip, he said 'Ok, I'm listening.'

'When Eloise said that we met at work, she was telling the truth; but what we didn't mention was how. She is an undercover journalist'

Hearing that I am an undercover journalist his father gave me a look that chilled me to the bone. Knowing about his distaste for crimes committed against women, how would he feel when he discovers that his own son has been accused of trafficking and abusing them?

'who, after being given an anonymous tip off about sex trafficking from the club decided to pose as a waitress at Bar 21 in London. At the same time as she received her tip off, we received one about her, including a complete dossier on her life as if a private investigator had been following her for some time. There were documents showing her real and fake identities, pictures showing her home address, the vehicle she drove, even a plan of the layout of her home. There were also documents relating to our activities that she was actively investigating, and her daily routines; what time she gets up and goes to bed, the time she leaves for work, the route she travels, where she shops, who her friends are, the gym she uses and the times she attends, etcetera, you get the picture.'

Someone had been following me? How had I not noticed? Someone had delved so deeply into my life, giving Dalton everything he needed to plan the perfect abduction.

'Naturally when I saw her working at the club, I decided to pay her a visit, she was getting too close for comfort and I needed to warn her off,' Dalton empties his glass and begins to pour another one before continuing, 'however, to safeguard our interests, I decided to bring her back with me, to extract any information she had discovered, and to find out if she had told anyone else,' looking at me I shake my head to indicate that I hadn't told anyone anything, because despite trying, there was no sex trafficking story there. 'Our tech guys trawled through everything on her laptop, trying to find a paper trail, making sure that no damage had been done to us. They didn't find any information relevant to any of our business ventures but they did find some pictures of a man on her laptop. The same day that she arrived here, we received another letter demanding that we return his daughter, or there would be a war, she later confirmed that the pictures we had found were of her father.' Tears began to form in Daltons eyes, sorrow for the truth he must tell his father, and sorrow for what mine had done. 'Father, this will not be easy for you to hear, but I must tell you; most of the families are already aware thanks to the spy we have in our midst. Eloise is the daughter of Eduardo Mendez.'

Throughout Daltons explanation to his father of the circumstances around my arrival into their lives, and who my father is, I watch the conflict of emotions play across his fathers face, from amusement of how we had initially met, and Daltons decision to abduct me, to confusion over the photos and the relevance of other crime families being aware of my existence, finally settling on anger after discovering my true identity. Seeing the cold hard stare of absolute anger and hatred that he shoots in my direction, I shrink back in the sofa, trying to make myself as small and insignificant as possible. He is staring at me so intently, searching my features, and looking for any bearing of resemblance to the man who had murdered his wife.

'Why of all people have you chosen to marry the daughter of the man who murdered your mother? You have been sent many suitable women to marry, those who would cement our future, and expand our empire, protecting us from any wars in the years to come,' His anger is apparent and spittle flows from his mouth as he speaks. He has not once looked at his son during his tirade, continuing to stare in my direction, as if staring right through me.

In this moment I really do not want to exist, the anger, which was to be expected when his father discovered the truth, was frightening. Dalton scared me at times, with Marcus scaring me the most, but his fathers anger was on a whole new level, I cannot remember ever being so afraid in my whole life. Bearing in mind in the past month or so, I have been through more than most.

'I have no choice,' Daltons voice was so quiet, it was barely audible, if it hadn't been for the fact that you could cut the silence with a knife, I very much doubt that he would have been heard at all.

'You have no choice? Preposterous! Of course you have a

choice; you are Dalton Mercedes, head of one of the wealthiest and most respected crime families in the world,' locking me with a death stare, he stands and moves towards me, his father is in such a rage, I very much doubt that Dalton will be able to calm him, let alone protect me if he chooses to attack, or orders one of his minions to do so. Marcus witnessing the escalation of Ricardos anger, moves away from the door and stands next to me. Ricardos eyes are filled with rage, I honestly believe that he no longer sees me, and instead it is the image of my father sitting in front of him.

Dalton stands and walks towards him, 'Father, sit down, I will not let you hurt her. I will not let you do something that you will later regret.'

'I will only tell you this once' his father looks directly at Dalton, pausing for affect on every word 'Get Rid Of Her!'

Dalton shaking his head, says painfully 'If only that were an option'

I am shocked; he would send me away, he would set me free if he could? He doesn't want to marry me, anymore than I want to marry him. A small glimmer of hope begins to surface, I could be free, free to live, love and laugh. I wouldn't have to remain a prisoner and forced into a marriage of convenience. Seeing this as my opportunity to be set free, I begin to plead my case.

'It is an option, just drop me off somewhere, I won't say a word about any of this, I promise.'

'No!' Dalton interrupts me before I am able to fully divulge my plan of release. Sitting next to me he wraps his hands around mine, looking deep into my eyes, whispering, 'it isn't an option.'

I look imploringly at his now seated father, hoping that he will at least give me the opportunity to be heard, but it is as if I haven't even spoken, my very existence was lost on the man as soon as he discovered my heritage.

'Why isn't it an option? Explain, and this had better be good, or I will be taking her with me tonight and returning her to her father as requested. You know full well that we are in the middle of a very lucrative deal at the moment, and we cannot afford a war over some stupid girl. You may run the business, but I am the head of this family. I am in charge and what I say goes.'

Stupid girl, I have never been so incensed before, I am anything but stupid. I worked extremely hard to gain my degree in Journalism; growing up in the care system wasn't easy, moving from one abusive home to another you struggle to form attachments to people, attending college and leaving the care system at 18, having to apply for university funding and housing. My life has been anything but easy, and being called a "Stupid Girl" just about pips the post.

'I am not sure if you are aware, but we have suspected for some time that there is a spy living on the Island. We have been trying to track him down, but so far he remains elusive. The information that was being leaked was petty nonsense, it would not have harmed our operations in any way, which is why we didn't put everything we had into pursuing them; that is until Eloise arrived. Since her arrival, the information that has been shared centres solely around our relationship. Not only to our enemies; but also to the enemies of her father, those that are loyal to us, some want to use Eloise to hurt her father; others want to use her because they believe that it would hurt me.'

'Why would they believe that it would hurt you?' his

father appears to be calming down after his initial outburst, attentively listening to the facts around the predicament we currently find ourselves in.

'We were seen together; before I discovered who her father was, and then when I brought her back from the Cabin,' pausing as he remembers the state that I had managed to get myself into during my time there, 'when I discovered who her father was, I sent her there, partly because I could not bear to look at her, partly because I wanted to show the spy that I didn't care about her, and I also wanted to run a background check into her story. I couldn't do that while she was around.'

His father, looking from Dalton to myself whilst nodding his head, 'the information that has been leaked is hearsay; deny it, send her away and move on with your life, find a more suitable bride.'

'There are pictures; some of us in the garden,' looking at the floor, colour beginning to flood his face, whilst continuing, 'but mostly of us, in her, I mean, in moms apartment.'

If the pictures are of us in the apartment, that can only mean one thing; someone has taken photos of us whilst we were in the throws of primal passion. I can feel the bright red colour of pure embarrassment flood my face as the meaning behind his words hit me. Looking at the floor I cannot bring myself to look at any of the three men in the room.

'I do not understand, there have been pictures of you before; it hasn't previously posed an issue for you.' Daltons father has leaned forward, placing his elbows on his knees, trying to get to grips with the true situation.

'There have been threats made against her, some are quite descriptive in what they would like to do to her,' Dalton released my hand, and poured himself another glass of amber liquid. 'Marcus, please give the file to my father.'

I hadn't even spotted the manila file being held against his side until Dalton had brought my attention to it. Fascinated, I watched the progress of the folder as it was placed on the table in front of us.

Daltons father, picks it up, and opens it carefully, flicking through the pages; spending longer on some sheets then others, his eyes flicking left to right as he read the information on each one. Others were flicked over quickly, making me assume that they were the pictures that had been mentioned, heat flooding my face once again. His fathers face was unreadable as he continued looking at the information in front of him.

When he had finally finished, he closes the file and places it on the table, pushing it towards Dalton, looking at me with pity, 'I think I am beginning to understand now'

Looking at the file on the table so close to my grasp, and hearing the acceptance in Daltons fathers voice, I decide that I need to know what was contained in the thick manila folder. Whilst they were both occupied draining the contents of their glasses I reach for the file. I already know that Dalton has lightening quick reflexes, if he really doesn't want me to see the contents, he could easily stopped me. The folder is on my lap; I pause for a second, trying to muster up the courage to turn the front cover. As I had reached for the folder, my mind was made up, that I wanted to know what it contained; what information was inside that had made Daltons father change his stance on our upcoming wedding. But now the opportunity was in front of me, I couldn't decided if actually I wanted to know the truth behind the threats against me, they do say that ignorance is bliss. But perhaps if I was reprised of all of the information, it would make what I was being forced to do more appealing. Decision made, I begin to open the folder, as if in slow motion Dalton places his hand on top of the folder, stopping it in its progress.

'Eloise, I wouldn't recommend you looking inside, but if you feel you must know the truth, I will not stop you.'

Suddenly feeling appreciated and able to make my own decisions, well one decision at least, I look into his eyes, the pain and fear inside them on display for me to see, 'I have to know, I'm sorry.'

Accepting my need for information, he removes his hand allowing me to look inside. Flipping open the cover, I saw a typed sheet detailing my life; my date of birth, but the names of my parents are missing for whatever reason, the college and university I had attended, the qualifications that I had achieved, my home address, details of the car I drove, pictures of my true and fake identities, along with clippings of some of the pieces I had written in the past.

'This, along with the next sheet, is from the first tip off we had.'

All of the information was pretty accurate, it didn't cover my childhood or who my parents were, but I guess accompanied with the following sheet it would have been enough to peak the interest of anyone.

The next sheet detailed the supposed investigation I was running against his family, it showed pictures of me in various places, camera in hand, snapping eagerly away. Whilst it was true that I was present at these places, the topic of the investigation was completely different; Dalton had been told that I had received information pertaining to a huge shipment of cocaine, being brought into the country, which was going to be used as payment for merging two notorious crime families together; the Mercedes clan being one of them, and for paying off public service workers to turn a blind eye when further shipments landed. Obviously if this deal was taking place, my part in investigating it would have had a huge impact on the finances and notoriety of the family.

The next ten or so sheets were much of the same, dates and times of my movements, along with picture evidence to back this up. The fact that someone had gotten so close to me; detailing every minute of my life, whilst I was none the wiser, filled me dread. They had gotten so close to me; they could have even been a friend or colleague.

The next sheet was very similar to the first, but had more details of my movements, where I frequented during my leisure time, where and what I liked to eat, where I bought my weekly shopping, who my friends were, the tube I'd take and the times. My life laid bear on paper; I can't help but think, that apart from my house, which is now a pile of ash, I have nothing to show for my life.

'This is the report from our Private Investigator, there are also some pictures; you will notice that in some they are taken at the same time, but from different angles. You were being followed by at least two people and you didn't even realise. How can I do what you ask and set you free, you would be dead, or worse, in less than a week.'

'What's worse than death?' I can't help but ask, because surely death is the worse thing that can happen to you.

'Keep looking through, it will all become clear to you,' the look on his face is grim, making me second-guess myself, and whether I really wanted to know the answers to all of the questions swimming in my mind.

Looking from Daltons expression, back to the pieces of paper on my lap, I muster the courage and continue to flick through. The next sheet has letters cut out from newspapers and magazines, using various sizes, font styles and colours, they spelled out; "Return my daughter, or there will be a war!" with a picture of me leaving the plane after we had landed on the island.

Another sheet said much the same, ordering him to return me, failure to do so would result in consequences for anyone associated with him.

The next few sheets were pictures taken in quick succession of both of us, the night we had shared dinner, we were in the garden, looking at each other, before he kisses me, and I take his hand leading him inside. The fact that someone had gotten so close to us, somewhere where we should feel safe, was unimaginable. The next sheet, same childish cut out letters, "So she's your weakness? My plans for her will bring you, and your empire to its knees"

I quickly turned the following pictures over, refusing to focus on them, heat flooding my face, when I realised that there were at least ten pictures showing our first night together, another newspaper cutting letter, "I see you are training her up for me. I can't wait to show her how much Daddy has missed her"

This spy had gotten really close, what steps, if any, has Dalton taken to stop this happening again. Is this why I was placed in the apartment of his mother when I returned from the cabin? I also can't recall seeing the two guards that were initially on duty at the door of the bedroom I was placed in, on first arriving.

More photos followed; showing my eviction from the mansion, my arrival at the Cabin, and then when Dalton arrived to rescue me and bring me back here.

There were print outs of emails, I suspect from the families loyal to Dalton; asking for an explanation for my presence, and requesting that I am delivered to them; so that they can send my father a message once and for all. A graphic account of the abuse and torture that they wish to inflict. I shivered at the thought that someone could even sink this low to think these things up. But turning the sheet I realised that this was nothing compared to what my father wanted to do to me.

"I am so pleased that you are enjoying my daughter, some would say that she was made for you. So pretty, you could almost compare her to your mother. If you do not return her to me, I will take her, when you least expect it, it could be next week or it could be in ten years. You will lower your guard and she will be gone. I have built a special room for her, with padded walls - no one will hear her screams. When my men and I have finished using her, she will be sent around the world to be used by all of your enemies. Don't worry, when she has served her purpose, she will be returned to you, albeit in pieces, but eventually you will have all of her."

Shaking, I drop the sheet of paper; unable to fathom the hatred my father has for Dalton and his family, that he would use his own daughter for retaliation. A hatred that runs so deep he would inflict abuse and suffering on his own flesh and blood. Suddenly feeling sick, I stand, running towards the door with my hand over my mouth, wondering if I will make it back to the apartment in time before my stomach contents is forcibly evacuated from my body. Dalton clicks his fingers, and Marcus, as if understanding, is at my side, guiding me to the nearest toilet, which was lucky, as I only just made it in time.

Marcus shows his softer side, as he moves stray tendrils of hair off of my face, whilst rubbing my back, 'sshhh, it's ok, it will all be ok, don't worry, ssshhh'

When I have finished emptying my stomach contents; I continue to kneel, gripping the toilet seat, unable to move, as the realisation of the full danger I am in has now been shown to me. I begin to wail uncontrollably, deep sobs racking my body, holding onto the toilet seat so tightly as if it was an anchor and my life depended on it.

Marcus continues rubbing my back and talking soothingly to me. For a man that once scared me so much that I fainted, I am amazed that I find his softer side so comforting.

'Marcus, it's ok, I've got her' hearing the commotion that I was creating, Dalton and his father had come to help, 'Mi pequeno pajaro, please stop this. You will be ok, you will be safe, and you have my word that I will not let anything happen to you.'

'How?' is the only word I can formulate, how can he keep me safe, there are so many people wanting a piece of me, quite literally, I can see no way for him to make sure that I remain safe.

'Let us go back to the office; I'm sure you'd find it more comfortable than the bathroom floor. Father, please make your way back to the office; we will meet you there in a minute or so. Marcus please wait outside the door for Eloise,' after both men are given their orders and they depart, Dalton helps me to my feet, guiding me to the washbasin he removes a flannel from the vanity unit and begins to wipe my clammy face, placing another cool flannel on the back of my neck. Offering me a glass of water to swill my mouth out and then some minty mouthwash. Satisfied that I am no longer in meltdown mode, he turns me into a soft embrace, resting his head on top of mine,

'Mi pequeno pajaro, I promise that I will do everything in my power to keep you safe' before placing a small soft kiss on my full lips, 'come, we had better get back to my father, he doesn't like being kept waiting.'

Taking my hand, we leave the bathroom, two of my guards move to walk in front of us as he leads me back to his office; and Marcus falls in to follow closely behind us. On the way back to the office, I notice that there are a few more guards dotted around the house, they are in a slightly different uniform, so I assume that this is the guard detail for his father; as we walk past them they follow discreetly behind us. Not for the first time I think, "overkill" but then I remember the danger I am in and the threats made against me, and I find that I am actually thankful for being surround by these armed men, who would lay down their lives to keep me safe.

Settling in the same seats, I decide to pour myself a very large glass of brandy, draining the glass in one movement, I begin to cough uncontrollably as the liquid burns my throat on the way down, as soon as it hits my stomach I feel a warm glow start to radiate through my body. When the coughing subsides I ask, 'so what's the plan you've concocted?'

Dalton grins slightly at my slurred speech, somewhat amused at the immediate effect that the alcohol has on me, 'the only plan we could agree that would work, and keep you safe, would be for us to get married. All of our allies would tow the line, and would not dare to touch you, no matter how much they hate your father. We have a large team of private investigators working around the clock; trying to track him down, and when they do, we will neutralise the threat. Then and only then you can be set free if you still wish it.'

'But how will they know that we're even married? They could say that it has been faked.' Choosing to ignore that Dalton means to neutralise the threat my father poses to me by killing him.

'Because everyone has been invited, if they value their lives they will attend'

'Wow, so they have two choices, come to our sham wedding or loose their lives, tough choice.'

The darkness clouding Daltons eyes had me wondering what I had said wrong, I had merely stated the facts.

'If they do not come, it means that they are no longer loyal to us, which in turn means that they will be removed from the equation' this was the first time that Daltons father had spoken since we entered the office, 'when you get a request from Dalton Mercedes you follow it through, failure to do so has great implications.'

'Father, enough' Dalton is becoming increasingly agitated, but I cannot work out why. If we are to be married, I really need to get to grips with his mood swings.

'She needs to know what she is getting herself into, she needs to know that you are the head honcho of some of the most influential crime families globally. If she decides to go through with this marriage, she needs to be aware that there are other threats out there, yes it minimises the current ones somewhat, but there will always be some lurking in the background.'

'They will be dealt with in due course; my main priority is dealing with the one that is right in front of us. It is my fault that she has been put in this danger, if I had ignored the tip off then none of this would be happening. I am solely responsible.'

Hearing the resignation in his sons voice, knowing that his mind is made up and that the discussion on this topic is now closed, Ricardo rises to his feet, 'it is late, and I am tired. I presume that my quarters are as I left them.' Dalton inclines his head in confirmation, 'In that case, I will retire to bed. Eloise, as you will soon become my daughter, I would very much like to get to know you better, I will join you for breakfast tomorrow. I will be with you at 9 o'clock. Good night'

Watching Ricardos proud figure as he walks away from us, I realise that he had virtually ordered me to have breakfast with him. Perhaps despite seeing all the evidence to the contrary, he still didn't complete trust me, and still thought of me as a gold digger.

Feeling Daltons arm around my waist as he pulls me towards him, and kisses me with such passion and urgency, as if it had been too long since his cock was last invading me. Hitching my dress up my thighs, he manoeuvres my position so that I am straddling him. I could already feel the heat of his rock-hard cock as he pulls me towards him, holding my arse as he gyrates his hips towards me.

The sound of the office door closing with a quiet click as Marcus discreetly leaves the room, makes us both freeze, we quickly realise that we had forgotten about his presence. Embarrassment floods my cheeks, the thought of having to walk past him to get back to the apartment filling me with dread. How could I have been so stupid to forget that he was there; was

Daltons power over me so great that I would forget the simplest of things?

Dalton begins chuckling to himself; apparently he finds the fact that we were almost practically fucking in front of Marcus, highly amusing. His chuckle gets louder as he begins a proper belly laugh, it was contagious and I couldn't help but join in, my embarrassment quickly forgotten.

Once we have managed to get our laughter under control, tears streaming down our faces, Dalton looks directly into my eyes, the passion and lust that he still has for me is clearly evident, and if I am honest with myself I feel the same way. I cannot guarantee that I can live my life a prisoner of our combined lust for each other forever, but for now it will have to do.

Carrying me back to the apartment, he sets me down on the floor in lounge; cupping my chin gently he places a small kiss on my lips. 'Eloise, I want you so badly that it hurts. But I also want our wedding night to be one that you will never forget, for this reason, and this reason alone I will not touch you again until after we are married.' Turning on his heels, he leaves the apartment through the same door we have just entered it by.

The mound of nerves between my legs is throbbing so badly that it hurts, I want him inside of me and I cannot quite believe that he intends to refrain from touching me until after our wedding; it will be pure torture for the both of us.

SEVEN

Considering all of the facts being laid out to me in black and white the previous evening, I wake feeling refreshed after a surprisingly restful sleep. Arching my back as I stretch, I turn my head when I sense Daltons presence close by. My eyes rest on him sitting in the armchair that he has moved away from the window so he can sit as close to the bedside as possible. The boyish grin he gives me as he stretches, tells me that he has been sitting there for a while.

'Morning, Mi pequeno pajaro, my father will be down for breakfast shortly, if you are quick you will have time to have a shower.'

Checking the time on the clock next to the bed, I realise that I actually have very little time to get ready, jumping out of my bed I run into the bathroom, switching on the shower and brushing my teeth, as the temperature of the water gets hot enough for me.

Stepping underneath the hot running water I quickly wash my hair and body, taking special care to not be too rough with my hair, as I do not have time to detangle millions of knots this morning. Drying myself as I walk towards the dressing room, I spy Dalton sitting in the same position, watching me intently with a small smile on his face. He is obviously finding it somewhat amusing that I have overslept and am now rushing around like a mad thing.

Selecting an outfit that I hope is appropriate to meet his father for breakfast, I hear Dalton chuckling from the bedroom.

Poking my head around the doorframe with an eyebrow raised, 'what's so funny?'

Still smiling to his self, 'I'm sorry, I couldn't help myself, and I set your clock forward by an hour. I was curious how quickly you could get ready if you put your mind to it.'

'Seriously, that is not even funny Dalton, for gods sake.' Approaching the bed I pick up one of the feather pillows and hit him over the head with it. Laughing in delight as he pulls it away from my grasp, I instantly find myself against his hard body, his mouth crashing into mine, I can feel his cock grinding against my abdomen, as his hands begin their frantic searching of my body. The flutters of my lust rising to the surface, hoping that he will take me, and drive his cock deep inside of me, making me scream his name in ecstasy.

All of a sudden, he stops kissing me back, placing his hands on my waist he pushes me away from him, 'we can't do this, I'm sorry.'

Seeing the hurt at his rejection in my eyes, he cups my face and places a lingering kiss on my cheek.

'Be patient, I promise you it will be worth the wait. Let's talk outside, I'm less likely to ravish you if we have an audience.' Leading me through the doors to the enclosed garden, I see that a tray of coffee, with two cups have been placed on the patio table. Pouring a cup for each of us, before handing one to me, and sitting in one of seats, I sit opposite him trying to read his face for some inkling of what he is thinking. Wondering if he wants to continue the conversation from last night.

Taking a sip of the hot coffee, I look at him, waiting for him speak.

'Tell me about your childhood, after your parents were murdered.'

'You mean my mothers murder, we both know that my father is still alive.' Not wishing to revisit the fact that my father is still alive, but I need to face the truth that he is, and means to harm me in the most vicious of ways.

'You are right, he is, but the way I see it, the man who you thought your father was also died that night' as soon as he said this, I realise that he is right. My father did die that night, only to be replaced with a monster.

'I don't really remember much about the night that it happened, and it is only recently that I have been having flashbacks. After it happened, the trauma caused my brain to shut down, and I was unable to speak for a while. Through kindness and counselling I slowly regained my voice, but the memory of that night was gone.'

'Do you remember much about your life before it happened?'

'Not really, there are images and clips, but I couldn't tell you if they are real or my mind made them up. I believe that my mother looked very similar to me, but I have no family photos to prove it.'

Nodding, as if he is deep in thought, 'Who raised you and took care of you afterwards?'

'As I have no living family I was brought up in the care system, shoved from one foster family to another. None of them being able to cope with me for very long, as a child I suffered from terrible nightmares, which would disturb the rest of the home. A few people made inquiries about adopting me, but they always fell through after reading my file. It would appear that no one wanted the hassle of taking on a damaged child. Why are you asking all of this of me? I really don't like reliving my past.'

'I am just curious about your life, there is some things that our Private Investigators were unable to discover, I am just trying to fill in the blanks. They have still been unable to track down your birth certificate, it appears that before you were six or seven, Eloise Mansell didn't even exist.'

'What do you mean that I didn't exist? Of course I existed, I went to school, I had friends and I had parents who loved me.' I can feel the lump in my throat as I force back the tears that are trying to spring from my eyes, reliving my childhood makes me realise how unhappy it actually was.

'Please don't cry Mi pequeno pajaro,' reaching out to hold my hand, but withdrawing it just as he gets near, as if he doesn't trust himself to touch me. 'I don't mean to upset you. I am trying to find out why your existence has been wiped away, I believe that whatever information your mother had, was so dangerous, that your father had to have her killed, and that in order to protect you, your identity was changed so well that there is no record of who you actually were. I would like to help you discover your birth name, and to trace any living family members that you may have.'

'So if I am not Eloise, who am I?' could I have a living relative, someone who would care for me, reminding myself of the amount of times I had been let down in the past I try not to get my hopes up. But if there is a chance that there is, surely I should try to find them.

'Senor,' Sophia interrupts us, standing in the doorway,

wringing her hands in worry.

What on earth could have made Sophia so worried; I couldn't recall seeing her like this before.

'Senor Ricardo,' was all that I could grasp as the rest of the conversation was spoken in Spanish, I really need to learn this language, at least then I would be able to understand what was being said about me.

'Si gracias Sophia. Come, my father is here for breakfast.' Rising to his feet, he offers me his hand, having second thoughts and dropping it to his side before I can reach out for it.

Are the unanswered questions centring on my childhood causing the change in his demeanour to me? Has he decided that offering me his protection through marriage is to high a price to pay?

Following Sophia and Dalton through the apartment towards ante-lounge, I can't help but stare at his behind, he really has an exquisite arse, I really want to reach out and take it in my hands, giving it a proper squeeze. Images of grabbing it whilst he slams his cock inside of me, making me scream in ecstasy, comes into my mind, the wetness in my pants tells me that I need to try to stop thinking like this. He has made it perfectly clear that he will not touch me until after we are married, and so far he has been true to his word, much to my disappointment.

Hearing our approach, Ricardo rises to his feet in greeting, 'Eloise, you look a delight my child, come and sit with me.'

After the facts about our situation were laid out in front of him last night, his attitude towards me has definitely changed, he appears to be quite welcoming, and accepting of the fact that I will soon be marrying his son, and becoming his daughter in law.

Sitting in the seat next to him, he passes me a small plate, indicating for me to help myself to the vast array of pastries and fruits laid out on the table in front of us. Reaching cautiously for a piece of fruit, I notice that Dalton and his father are staring at me, an unspoken message passes between them as they look towards each other, before his father looks at me again with pity in his eyes.

'What's going on? And don't tell there isn't anything, I know that something is.'

Ricardo removes an ear piece and places it on the table in front of him, 'I was listening to the conversation you were having with my son, please do not blame him, I ordered him to do it as I do not think that you would open up to me as well as you do with him.'

'Why is my childhood relevant to this situation? Surely you have been told everything you need to know.'

'Dalton merely asked for my help understanding you a little more.'

Looking at Dalton, who had fished into my past, which had caused me to relive some of the darkest times in my life, while the whole time he was feeding personal information to his father. I am suddenly feeling quite angry with the deceit of the Mercedes men in front of me, 'what do you need to understand so desperately that you would betray me like this. I told you that it isn't a subject that I am happy to discuss.'

'Mi pequeno pajaro, I am sorry, normally I would not ask for help, but I am so blinded by you I cannot think straight. I was hoping with my fathers help, I would be able to help you heal, so that you are no longer a victim to your nightmares or suffering with panic attacks. I did not betray you, I am trying to help you.'

'Regardless of your good intentions, I feel betrayed.'

'Eloise, I think I already know some of the answers to Daltons questions, so hopefully with our help you can discover who you really are, and why you react in certain ways to some situations'

'Really, so come on then Sigmund, what information did you pertain that would allow you to come to a credible conclusion.' Knowing that I sound like a rude spoilt brat, but I couldn't control the rage building inside of me any longer, I really didn't care if I upset either of them right now.

'Firstly, why despite the fact you are obviously hungry when food is laid out in front of you; you pick at it like a sparrow, ultimately starving yourself. The rest can wait?'

'I do not starve myself, I'm just not a very big eater.' I hadn't realised that every aspect of my life was being monitored to this extent. What can he possibly mean by "the rest?" I am, correction, was, perfectly happy until he barged into my life. Abducting me, making me want him so badly that I cannot think straight, and then to top it all off place me in so much danger that I am being forced to marry him.

'The small amount you eat is not enough to survive, judging by the photos that were taken of you on your arrival, you have lost an incredible amount of weight since then. I imagine that you must look emaciated underneath your clothes. Dalton is concerned that his actions have affected you in some way, but if you wish to starve yourself to death, I will not stand by and watch my son suffer alongside you. He may not have told you, but I know my son, and he cares for you a great deal. So stop torturing yourself and him.'

Deciding that I have had enough of being lectured over my eating habits, I rise and politely excuse myself, wishing for the privacy of my room, away from the controlling men in my life. Dalton moves to follow me, holding my hand up to stop his progression towards me, 'no, stay here, I just want to be alone.'

Deflated and worried that he has overstepped an invisible line, he sits in the chair that I have vacated, watching me as I leave the room, and close the door behind me. Sitting in the armchair next to his father, he wages an internal battle, unsure if he should disregard my request for privacy and follow me anyway.

His father places a supportive hand on his arm, 'leave her for now; she will be fine, eventually. You will have a lot of work in front of you to repair her physically and mentally; she is more damaged than I previously thought. Are you sure this is what you want? That you want to marry this girl?'

'I have already told you that I have no choice'

'My son, I know you better than you know yourself, I have loved you from the minute you were born and placed in my arms. You know as well as I do that if you didn't want to marry this girl, you would find a way out of it.'

'I cannot see another way, I'm sorry. I blame myself entirely, no one has forced me to take the actions that I have taken, I am responsible for her safety'

'Ok, that's the decision made then, when you are ready to admit your true feelings to me, let me know. I have some phone calls to make, I will see you at dinner.'

Standing to leave, Ricardo turns and looks at the sorrowful figure of his son, 'can I give you some advice, stay close to her, she will need your support now more than ever, for what is to come.'

As he leaves the apartment he nearly crashes into a flapping Magda, her excitement is palpable, as the wedding dress designer has arrived. Without stopping to speak to Dalton, she crashes through the apartment in search of Sophia, thankful that on hearing her I have time to return to my apartment. Yes, I feel slightly guilty listening in on the private conversation between Dalton and his father, but remembering that they have just done the same to me helps alleviate the feeling slightly.

Just as I manage to sit in the chair in my room, there is a hard knock at the door before Magda comes barging in, a whirlwind of excitement. I couldn't help but smile at this matronly woman, flapping a towel around her as she speaks excitedly, almost forgetting to draw breath.

Sophia follows on her heels, almost as excited as Magda, relaying, 'Dress, here now.'

'Sorry, what? What dress?' cruel I know, for I knew exactly what had caused all of the commotion.

Sophia, being her usual careful self, aware that there are ears everywhere, held me in a tight hug and whispered in my ear, 'the tailors are here to measure and make your wedding dress.'

Try as I might, I couldn't match their excitement and enthusiasm, I really just wanted to sit and divulge the conversation I had heard between Dalton and his father. What did he mean that I am damaged? I have never given and thought to this, but perhaps the trauma from my childhood has affected more than I have previously realised.

Plastering a fake smile on my face, 'great, I'd better go and get measured then' as Sophia takes my hand and leads me to the large lounge, which has been cleared of furniture; except for a small table and two chairs in one corner, allowing room for the bolts of fabric and lace on display.

A tall woman in her mid fifties greeted me with a warm smile as I enter the room. Despite her age, this woman was stunning with her jet-black hair pulled back into a tight bun, and dark brown eyes, framed with perfectly applied makeup. Taking in her elegant appearance, I feel very underdressed and completely out of my comfort zone.

'Good morning Eloise, it is so lovely to meet you. My name is Lucia, and I will be designing your dress, Senor Mercedes has made a few requests, so we will need to work around these. Have you given any thoughts to the colour or fabrics you would like to use.'

'Not really, this has all been a little rushed if I'm honest.'

Glancing quickly at my flat stomach, I realise that she has incorrectly assumed that, as the wedding is being rushed, that I must be pregnant. Realising that Dalton and I hadn't discussed the possibility of having children in the future, mainly because we can't keep our hands off of each other, but I know that if I were ever to conceive his child, I would not want it to be raised living in constant fear of retribution. I would have to keep it a secret and either abort it, or escape.

Realising that Lucia is still talking to me, showing me the available fabrics, explaining how they would drape around my figure, I make a show of being interested. After selecting a pure white satin, we begin to place lace over the top, apparently this will give the dress some depth, whatever that means. Once the lace has been selected we move on to the rhinestones and crystals.

'Ok, that's enough for me to begin designing your dress;

we'll use this tulle for the veil as the colour will match the dress perfectly. Lets sit down so that I can show you some images of dresses, you can interchange the bodice and skirt if you wish.'

Taking a seat next to Lucia, she begins to show me hundreds of images of wedding dresses; I am so far out of my comfort zone. Most little girls grow up dreaming of their perfect wedding dress, when they marry their Prince Charming or Knight in Shining Armour, but as far as I can recollect, I never did. Thinking of the man that I will be marrying and I couldn't class him as either, he was more like a Devil in disguise, and I can't help thinking that in going through with this wedding, I am making a deal with the Devil himself.

With great difficulty, and a lot of cajoling by Lucia, we decide on a dress design. It will have a sweetheart neckline with a lace halter-neck overlay, the back will be open with a love heart cut out, with a fitted skirt that splays out at the bottom forming the train, and teamed with a cathedral veil that will extend beyond the hem of the dress. Lucia seems very pleased with the selection, and was constantly telling me how divine I will look.

Whilst Lucia begins to sketch the finished gown, a gentleman, who introduces himself as Matteo, takes the relevant measurements to enable the dress to be made. Not for the first time I think to myself that this is overkill, considering that this is a sham marriage I would prefer a discreet, quiet wedding: the amount of effort that is being put in to it at the moment, seems like an extravagant waste of money.

Looking at the finished sketch, I was beginning to feel a small amount of excitement bubbling below the surface. The dress, when it is made will look simply stunning, and I can't wait to try it on. Feeling slightly sad that I am more excited about having a gorgeous dress than I am about having a gorgeous husband in a few days time.

I watch with fascination as a small army of seamstresses enter the room, setting up a makeshift factory with several sewing machines. Taking this as my cue to leave them to it, I walk towards the door leading to the hallway and the confines of my bedroom. Desperately wanting some peace and quiet, the sheer amount of noise and people playing on my fractious nerves.

'Eloise, I'm sorry but we need you to stay with us.' Lucia calls after me, although it was a simple request, her tone made it sound more like an order.

Adding her to the list of people, who were ordering me around and trying to control me every aspect of my life, I could feel myself become angry; not just towards Lucia, but towards everyone that had crossed my path since my audition at Bar 21. Since then my life has been turned upside down.

'What on earth for? Surely you have everything you need,' continuing in my progress to leave the room.

'Not quite, we still need to discuss your tiara and jewellery; I have several options to show you. Please come and sit with me so I can show you the selection.'

Feeling slightly badgered, but wanting to get this over with as quickly as possible, I sit next to her, and choose the first one she shows me.

'Wonderful choice, you are going to look simply divine,' although I don't quite believe her and am beginning to feel that this is just a ploy to keep me in this room. Something is obviously happening elsewhere that I am not allowed to be party to. More secrets and lies in order to protect me, do they really believe that I am so frail that I am unable to deal with anything?

Lucia checking her watch for the umpteenth time, 'The jeweller will be with us shortly, so you can select the rings that you will present to each other.'

'Well, all this excitement has made me very tired,' if they think I am this frail thing then I may as well play on it, 'ask Sophia to come and get me when he arrives.'

'No, you must stay here.' Lucia seems frantic with worry, what on earth is going on.

'Why?' my voice comes out quite forceful, demanding to know why I must not leave this room.

'Senor Mercedes has told me to keep you here' my tone shocks Lucia into telling me the truth, so they must have told that they believe that I am fragile, and to treat me with kid gloves.

'I repeat, why? What is going on?' I am determined to get to the bottom of this, either she tells me what's going on, or I will find someone who will.

'I cannot, erm, I mean, I don't know. Just that Senor has requested that you stay here' she's mumbling, grasping at lies to cover up the admission she almost made.

'Fine, if you won't tell me, I'll find someone that will. I do not like being lied to.'

Standing to leave, I come face to face with Dalton as he opens the door. His face telling me that he is worried about something, but seeing me looking at him, he quickly plasters a smile on as he walks towards me.

What is he hiding? Has there been another threat made against me? Have they found the spy? Whatever it is, I feel that I have a right to know.

'What's happened?'

'Why would you think that something has happened?'

'Because Lucia has done everything she can to keep me in this room, apparently on your orders, and you looked worried when you opened the door just now.' Aware that our conversation may be overheard, I drop my voice, 'has there been another threat?'

'No, nothing like that at all, don't worry. I just have a few problems that I need to take care of. Lucia, do you have everything you need? I would like my fiancé to join me for lunch.'

'Um, yes, yes of course, we can send Sophia to find her if we need her.'

Judging by the flush on Lucias face I am almost certain that she was listening in to our conversation, obviously intrigued as to why one of the most eligible bachelors in the world is choosing to have a shotgun wedding with a nobody.

Hooking his arm around my waist he leads me to the small sitting area, the table is laid for three people with freshly made scones, fresh clotted cream, strawberry jam, finger sandwiches and a selection of cakes.

'I thought that as you spent some of your childhood in Devon, you might like an afternoon tea, Magda wasn't very happy making it, but when she discovered that it was for you, well as you can see, I think she has outdone herself.'

I couldn't help but be touched by his thoughtfulness, so much so that the smile on my face was real. Deep down I know that it was born out of worry over the small amount that I eat, but the fact that he is trying to entice me was heart warming. Jumping into his arms, I place my hands around his neck, kissing him deeply on this mouth. Hoping that he will kiss me back, and stop torturing us both.

Hearing him groan in frustration, 'please, don't, I am trying very hard to control myself, and you are not helping the situation. Just know that I want you as badly as you want me, nothing has changed in that regard' he places his hands on my waist and pushes me away slightly, but not quickly enough for me not to feel the size of his arousal, caged in his trousers.

Arching my eyebrow slightly, I look suggestively at the obvious bulge below his waistline. My efforts break the tension that has built around us as he chuckles to himself, whilst indicating for me to be seated in front of the delicious cream tea laid out before us.

Taking his seat, he picks up a scone, inspecting it with curious eyes, before smelling it and taking a large bite.

A burst of uncontrollable laughter filled the air as a look of disgust came on his face.

'This is disgusting, it's so dry, no wonder it is served with cups of tea,' grinning at me as he drops crumbs on the pristine white table cloth.

Chuckling to myself, my laughter under control, I explain to him, 'that's because you are doing it wrong. Look, watch me, you cut the scone in half, a large of dollop of cream and a spoonful of jam,' he watches with fascination as I load half of one of the scones with a healthy helping of cream. 'This is the Devonian way, the Cornish way has the jam going on first and then the cream on top. Here try it now.' Passing him the scone that I had loaded up for him, I watched as he takes a suspicious bite, watching with glee as his face changes, showing his appreciation of one of my favourite childhood treats. Loading the second half with cream and jam, I sit back and begin to devour the sweet, sticky mess; jam and cream dribbling down my chin, making Dalton shoot me his best boyish grin.

Hearing the sound of an engine overhead, I watch in fascination, as a helicopter gets closer to the house, it was so close to our position that I could clearly see the pilot speaking into the microphone he was wearing. Reminiscent of a scene in an action movie, just before they open fire and decimate everything in their path. I begin to stand, and look around, trying to work out where would be the safest place to hide. Knowing deep inside that this is not normal behaviour, most people wouldn't automatically assume that someone has sent a helicopter to kill them.

Seeing my distress at the scene unfolding in front of us as the helicopter begins to land on the lawn at the front of the house, Dalton holds my hand, gently rubbing his thumb on the inside of my wrist, trying to break the trance I am in.

'Eloise, it's ok, calm down, I promise nothing will harm you. Our guests have begun to arrive for our wedding, that is all.'

I can feel the tingle on my wrist that his touch is causing, and I can hear his calming voice, but my fear is so great I cannot snap myself out of the trance I am under. I am completely frozen, and unable to move, watching the helicopter land, deposit its passengers before climbing into the sky and flying away, to become a small speck on the horizon.

Hearing a plate smash on the marble floor next to me, snaps me out of it almost instantly, but causes Dalton to jump, making him turn to look at Sophia as she bends to pick up the fragments.

'Sophia, what the hell?' Dalton is suddenly angry at being caught unawares in his efforts to reach me.

Sophia simply shrugs her shoulders, and nods at me, 'it work.' Once she is satisfied that she has collected all of the fragments, she rises and leaves the room.

Dalton glances at me, realising that he is still holding my hand and rubbing my wrist, causing shock waves to travel up my arm, and settling at the cluster of nerves between my legs. My arousal is obvious to him as I look at him with parted lips, waiting for him to claim them.

Hearing footsteps approach the apartment door, he drops my hand as if it would burn him, but my arousal is still there, the tell tale signs clearly evident on my flushed cheeks. Watching Dalton lean towards me, with passion and lust in his eyes, I am almost sure that he is going to claim my lips, in my mind he carries me to the bedroom before giving us what we are both so desperately craving. Hearing Magda come crashing through the door he looks away briefly, when he looks back towards me the mask is firmly in place.

He looks at Magda, while she begins her tirade in Spanish, as someone begins to lay an extra setting at the table in front of us. It would appear that there are an extra two people joining us for afternoon tea. Wondering whom it could be as a look of anger crosses Daltons face, and he begins to berate and argue with Magda.

'Si, Senor, el esta aqui y quiere verla.' I notice that Magda is still flapping her tea towel around as she speaks; I suppose some people speak with their hands, whilst Magda speaks with her tea towel.

'No, es muy pronto' I can feel the anger rippling off of Dalton as he stands, looking down a Magda, who shows no sign of backing down or fear.

'Tu Padre dijo que esta bien'

I watch in fascination, wondering who will win this argument, but also curious as to the cause of it. With Magdas final impart, they both look down at me, Daltons anger and worry clearly evident, whilst Magda just looks resigned that whatever has taken place between them, that she has won.

Magda, being satisfied that the table has been laid for our extra guest, bustles out of the room, sounding as if she is chastising herself as she goes.

'Disculpe Senor y Senor' as she nearly bumps into Daltons father, walking beside a man of a similar age and stature as himself.

Dalton strides towards his father and the mystery man, and meets them halfway, keeping his voice low, hoping that I will not here their conversation. 'Father, I told you no, this is too soon, I don't think she will be able to handle this on top of everything else.'

'How can she know who she is, if you continue trying to hide things from her? Do you really want to enter into a marriage full of deceit from the outset?'

'Are you one hundred percent sure that he is who we think he is? I will not allow you to hurt her.'

'Son, if I wasn't sure, I wouldn't be doing this. The DNA tests have confirmed it. Please let me handle this, you are too close to her and unable to read her reactions. I promise that I will handle her carefully, if I think that she isn't ready yet, I will wait until tomorrow before I tell her. Either way, she will know the truth before you say your vows.' Ricardo slaps Dalton on the back before approaching the table, the two men falling in to step behind him.

Bending down, he places a peck on each cheek, 'Eloise, you look stunning as always.' Looking at the afternoon tea laid out on the table, he looks questioningly at Dalton, 'what is this? I thought you said that we were having lunch, this isn't lunch, it's a Childs tea party.'

Laughing at the look of disgust on his face I explained, 'where I grew up this is called an Afternoon Tea, it is normally served as a special treat between lunch and dinner, but it works just as well for lunch.'

'I see, well I suppose seeing as you have tried our dishes, it would be rude of me not to try one of yours. Eloise, allow me to introduce you to an old family friend Juan Ramirez.'

Looking up at the gentleman before me, I hold out my hand, smiling as I say, 'Hello, it's nice to meet you.'

Taking my hand with a tear in his eye, he kisses it; without releasing my hand, he sits in the seat next to me, where Dalton was originally sitting. If Dalton was put out by this manoeuvre, he certainly doesn't show it, he simply sits across the table from me.

Watching Juan as he sits next to me, he is still showing no sign of releasing my hand, which is beginning to make me feel very uncomfortable.

'Juan, have a sandwich,' Ricardo orders, breaking Juan from the trance he is on.

Releasing my hand, he reaches for a plate and places a selection of sandwiches on it. I can feel his continual stare as he begins to take small bites of the sandwiches.

Dalton reaches for another scone and passes it to his father, 'Father, you have to try this cake, it is absolutely delicious' whist giving me a devilish wink, instantly removing the tension from the intense stare that I am being subjected to.

One bite of the dry scone caused the same reaction that Dalton had, except that his father walked to the bin and spat it out, making the three of us laugh. With tears rolling down my cheeks I patiently showed him how you should really eat a scone. He quickly decided that he preferred it when served properly; scowling at Daltons deception when I told him that he had done the exact same thing.

Curiosity makes me glance at the man, still staring at me whilst he is seated next to me. Looking at Dalton and his father, I can't help noticing that they are monitoring me intently, what on earth is going on, unable to stand the scrutiny from them any longer, I put on my journalist head and decide to get the answers to the questions floating around in my head.

'What's going on?'

'My child, why do you think something is going on? We are simply enjoying out afternoon tea, and taking in the views.' His facial expression does not match the words coming out of his mouth, he is quite clearly hiding something, they all are, and I plan to get to the bottom of it.

'For starters, none of you have stopped staring at me since you sat down, and Juan' glancing at the man next me, before looking back to look into Daltons fathers eyes, he may be good at detecting lies through the fluctuations of some ones pulse, but I can detect it in their eyes, 'is visibly upset by something, so something is quite obviously going on.'

'Eloise, this is a conversation for another time, can we not just enjoy each others company?' Dalton pleads with me, it is obvious to me that he is trying to protect me from something, but how can I feel safe if he insists on keeping something from me?

'No, whatever it is, clearly has something to do with Juan, seeing as we are all here, you may as well tell me. It seems pointless to delay it for another time.'

Juan chuckles next to me, 'so like her mother; forthright and determined.'

'Juan,' Dalton and his father bark at him in unison, unable to believe the statement that he has just made.

Turning to look at the old man, who was trying hard to stop the tears in his eyes running down his lined face, 'You knew my mother?'

'That's enough, lunch is over, Juan we are leaving,' Ricardo rises from his seat and throws his napkin on the table.

'Fine, you can go,' nodding at Juan, 'he stays. If he knew my mother I have a right to know. He could be my last link to recovering my memories of her.'

Hearing the determination in my voice, and somewhat amused at the way I had spoken to him, Ricardo sat back down in his seat, making it clear that he wasn't going anywhere. 'In that case if you insist on pursuing this, I feel it's only fair to remain, as there are some aspects of this that I am still unclear about.'

'Eloise, I knew your mother very well. I suppose that I should really start at the beginning, long before you were born' staring into space as he begins to regale me of his memories of the mother that I could no longer remember fully.

'Your mother was so beautiful; you look so much like her. She was a lot like you, kind, stubborn, determined and with a wonderful sense of humour, people would flock to her side knowing that she would defend them if needed. She was strong and courageous even though people thought that she was weak, but she was one of the strongest women I knew. She had numerous marriage proposals, men were eager to spend time in her company, she could have had her pick of suitable suitors, but unfortunately, she fell in love with your father. When I discovered this, I banned her from seeing him. Even all of those years ago, I knew that he had an evil streak, and I worried for her safety. We had an awful argument one night, she was pleading with me to give them my blessing, but even though she told me that she was expecting you, I couldn't give it. When I woke the following morning, she was gone, I never saw her again. Your father stole her from me, killing her and leaving you motherless.'

I couldn't believe what I was hearing, although I suspected what the answer was going to be, I couldn't help asking the question, 'who are you?'

'Eloise, I am your mothers father, your grandfather. If I had known of that you were still alive, then I would have moved heaven and earth to find you after her death.'

'Right, ok,' struggling to make my mind catch up with everything that I had learned in such a short space of time, deep down I am overjoyed that I have a family, a grandfather who professes to care for me. But after years of being let down I couldn't bring myself to believe it.

'Would you like to know what name your mother gave you on your birth?' he seems so pleased and excited that he has found me, yet I am still unable to match his enthusiasm, I just feel numb.

The years of growing up in care, being picked on in school for not having a mother, or not being able to wear the current fashions. There were no birthday parties, or friends coming over to play after school. Sadness begins to grow in my belly, knowing that it needn't have been this way, that my grandfather could have raised me with love, and kindness, if only he had known that I was still alive.

'Um I guess,' talking made the lump forming in my throat get bigger, fighting back the tears, eager to hear everything this old man has to tell me, my final link to my late mother.

'You were born "Samira Jade Ramirez", she named you Samira after her mother, and Jade because of the jade-blue colour of your eyes. I do not know why she didn't give you your fathers name, perhaps she was already realising that she had made a mistake. If only she had reached out to me I could have saved you both.'

Unable to listen to any more, the walls crushing in on me, the despair of the little girl inside of me screaming to be released, I stand and walk away, seeking out the quietness of my room.

Dalton rises with me, reaching for my hand, hoping that he hasn't lost me altogether.

Snatching it away from him, 'leave me alone, I just want to be alone right now.'

The three men watch my retreating back as I enter my room, I do not hang around hoping to listen in to their conversation, I have too much thinking to do with the information that I already have. Glancing over my shoulder, I see Dalton standing there watching me, the conflict on his face as he is unsure if he should follow me or not, waiting for me to give him a sign that I wanted him with me. Entering my room, I firmly close the door, sliding the lock into place behind me, thankful for my solitude.

I climb onto my bed and underneath the covers, burying my head into the pillow as screams of pain and anguish are finally released. I cry more tears than I thought was possible, the pillow soaking wet with them, but still the screams come from deep within me.

EIGHT

The sunlight hitting my face as it breaks through the clouds wakes me the following morning. Surprise registers when I realise that I have slept right through the night without a nightmare, and I look around the room, checking for evidence that Dalton has stayed with me again. Sadness hits me when I realise that he didn't stay with me last night, perhaps my rejection of him yesterday, had a more profound effect on him than I thought would be possible.

Placing my feet on the floor, I pad across to the door, checking that the bolt was still in place, and that Dalton had honoured my request to be left alone. Seeing that it was, I slide it open before crossing back to the en-suite, intending to soak my weary bones in a nice hot bath. I have barely made a few steps before the door opens, Dalton standing there looking distressed and as if he hasn't slept at all. Moving towards me slowly, as if afraid that he would spook me and I would run for cover, he reaches out and holds me face in his hands, searching it as if trying to read my thoughts.

'Mi pequeno pajaro,' placing desperate kisses on my face whilst whispering in Spanish, with tears trickling down is face. 'Lo siento, perdoname, lo siento mucho. Te quiero.'

Holding his face in my hands, I kiss him deeply on his lips, 'I'm fine, honestly I am. Thank you for finding him. I am going to have a bath and then find my grandfather,' as the word grandfather left my lips, I couldn't help but feel how alien it sounded to me.

'Now that you have found him, will you still want to marry me,' the sadness in his eyes pulls at my heartstrings, he looks like a lost little boy.

'I didn't think we had any choice, how would the fact that we've found him change anything.' What an unusual thing to ask, the whole time I have been told that we have to get married, and that there is no other way, and now that this old man has entered my life, everything has changed somehow.

'You don't know who he is do you?'

'Apart from him apparently being my grandfather, no I don't. Why who is he?'

'I should really let him explain. I will wait for you in the kitchen. When you are ready come and find me and I'll take you to him, he is staying in one of the cottages further inland.'

'Ok, thank you.'

Watching Dalton as he leaves, I can't understand the change in his attitude towards our marriage, I now have even more questions to ask the old man.

Although I really want a nice, long soak in a hot bath, I decide to have a shower. This way I will be able to meet and question him a lot quicker. In less than twenty minutes, I am walking into the kitchen, ready to visit my grandfather with Dalton. Seeing him slumped over his coffee cup at the table he looks so deflated, as if something has been taken away from him that he cannot get back.

'I'm ready, shall we go.'

Looking up, seeing me standing there, he plasters a fake

smile onto his face, 'are you going to have breakfast first, and before you say that you aren't hungry I need to remind you that you slept through dinner last night, you need to eat something.'

Grabbing an apple from the fruit bowl, and tossing it in the air before catching it and taking a large bite, 'satisfied? Come on, lets go,' my eagerness is apparent to him, and his shoulders slump forward a little more.

We walk to the front of the house, where three jeeps are waiting; two of them are heavily armed with machine guns mounted on their roofs. There are nearly a dozen armed men standing with the jeeps, their weapons are raised and they scan the surroundings, looking for imminent danger they are obviously on high alert.

My eyebrow arches, indicating to the armed escort, whilst smiling, hoping to break the tension that has arisen between us 'err, overkill do you think?'

Returning my smile, 'no, I don't, I cannot take any chances with your safety, not now that I have finally found you.'

Laughing at the look on his face, I place my arms around his waist and place a small kiss on his chin, 'thank you'

Guiding me to the second jeep, I sit in the back as Dalton climbs in next to me. Taking my hand in his and placing it in his lap, he absentmindedly rubs his fingers across my wrist, staring straight ahead, lost in his thoughts.

The journey doesn't take long, within five minutes we are pulling up outside another mansion, smaller than Daltons home, but a mansion none the less, why would they call this place a cottage? You could fit my house into it at least four times.

Marcus opens my door to allow me to exit the jeep.

'Marcus, can you give us a minute please.' Turning to me

as Marcus nods and closes the door, he holds me tight as he peppers small kisses across my brow line, my eyes and cheeks, finally coming to rest on my full lips, he kisses me with such sorrow as if he is saying goodbye to me. Pulling away, he cannot bear to look at me, and stares straight ahead, 'I will leave Marcus and the security detail here, they will bring you back later if you decide that that is what you want. Goodbye Mi pequeno pajaro.' With that he exits the jeep and climbs onto a waiting motorbike before speeding back to the house.

    Watching him as he speeds away, the sorrow he is feeling has mutated onto me. With a lump in my throat I turn and head up the winding path to meet with my Grandfather.

    'Eloise, I'm so pleased that you came, I wasn't sure if you would.' My grandfather enveloped me in a warm hug, it felt so nice being held by him. 'Lets go inside, I have some coffee and pastries prepared for you, Dalton informs me that you like them for breakfast.'

    So that is why there is always a selection of pastries available for breakfast; it would seem that his private investigator has told him of my morning routine of buying coffee and a pastry from a local coffee shop, it's a pity that he wasn't able to see that the pastry was actually for my boss. But even though the pastry wasn't for me, the fact that Dalton had gone to great trouble trying to make me feel as comfortable as possible made me smile. Looking at the engagement ring on my finger, I realise that the blue of the gemstone is the same colour as my eyes and the black is the same colour as his, is this another way of him telling me that he will always watch out for me?

    Being led by my grandfather through the house, I notice some family photos on the sideboards placed either side of the spacious corridor, pausing to look at them more closely, I notice the pictures were of a woman who looks so similar to me she could be my twin, judging by the age of the pictures I can only assume that she is my mother, in another one she is holding a baby, a bright smile on her face, there are a few more pictures showing the child grow into a toddler.

'That is your mother,' Juan points at the photo of the young woman holding a baby, 'and that is you. She sent this to me shortly after you were born, I received a photo of you once a year on your birthday, that is until you turned three.' Picking up the picture of a toddler running on the grass whilst blowing bubbles from a hoop, tears begin to well in his eyes. 'This is the last picture I have of you, I never heard from her again. I can only assume that your father discovered she had been secretly contacting me. If I had known that she was in trouble I would have protected her.'

I find it quite strange that this man would travel with family photos, sweet but peculiar at the same time, 'do you always travel with these?'

Looking down at me, he laughed slightly, 'no not at all, this is my house; the Mercedes family believe that all business associates should have their own homes on the Island, when visiting. Yes, granted, the main house is vary large and grand, and could easily accommodate everybody comfortably, but there is nothing like having your own space to call home.'

'You're his business associate? Exactly who are you?'

'Ah, Dalton hasn't told you has he? Well we'd better go and sit down, as this may take some time.'

Over the next few hours, Juan laid out his business dealings with the Mercedes family; he answered any questions that I had, truthfully and with patience. He is constantly assessing my reaction to the information that he is giving me; Dalton and his father have obviously told him of my previous panic attack and fainting episode. Marcus is hovering nearby, close enough to offer assistance but far enough away to afford privacy.

When Juan has finished divulging his information, I sit in silence for a while; processing everything he has told me.

'So let me get this straight, you are a business partner of the Mercedes family, and are one of the founding members of the alliance?'

'Correct, together Ricardo and myself put an end to the fighting that was happening between the different factions. Some would say that we bought peace to our industry, and saved a lot of lives.'

'So we are going to brush over the fact that the drugs you supply can kill people, shall we?'

'The product we supply is pure, so the unfortunate deaths that occasionally occur are from misuse. You could say that cars kill people, so does this mean that they should be made illegal? A car alone cannot kill a person; it is the person who is in charge of the vehicle that causes the death. It's the same with drugs, it is the person who is taking it wrongly that is responsible for their own death.'

'That is a really fucked up way of looking at it, but I guess in some aspects it makes sense.'

'Eloise, I would really prefer it if you didn't swear in my presence, it isn't very ladylike.'

'Yeah, sorry, I didn't have someone teaching me the etiquette of a conversation when I was growing up.' The second the words left my mouth I instantly regretted them, watching as the old man in front of me hung his head in shame for not being there for me. 'I'm sorry, I shouldn't have said that, sometimes I don't engage my brain before operating my mouth.'

Shrugging his shoulders and composing himself, he looked me in the eye, 'don't worry about it, it is true, you didn't have anyone as a child, but now you do. You have two men, in charge of two great families, ready to protect and fight for you.'

Looking at me as this sinks in, I realise that he is correct, I am at the centre of three men, waiting to wage a war over me, two wanting to protect me and keep me safe, the other wanting to use me to torture them.

'You need to decide what you want to do.'

'I don't understand, decide what?'

'Whether you really want to go through with your wedding to Dalton Mercedes tomorrow, I will not lie to you; from a business perspective it is a very good match, it would finally cement the alliance between our two families. But, I do not know if it is what is best for you; this is not an easy life, you will have to constantly look over your shoulder for threats; even after Eduardo has been found and neutralised. There will always be an opposing faction who will try to use you to overthrow Dalton, this is why we normally have arranged marriages, and it is less likely that a bond can be formed between the couple. By announcing his intention to marry you, he is announcing to the world that he cares for you a great deal.'

'But he doesn't, this is purely an arrangement to keep me safe.'

'You are so naïve if you believe that. If you decide that you no longer wish to marry him, you can leave the Island with me this evening; the Mercedes men will understand that everything has changed now. Or if you decide to go through with it, I would very much like to give you away tomorrow, if you would allow me to.'

I am astounded; I have so much information to process that my head is swimming with it, 'I think I need to go for a walk to think things through. Thank you for breakfast.' Rising to leave the table, Marcus is standing next to me in seconds.

'My dear, I am sorry but you are not able to walk the grounds yet, it simply isn't safe.' Looking at Juan as he closes his hand around mine, trying to pull me back into my seat.

Snatching it away from him, 'why isn't it safe? This is a private island.'

Marcus flashes a warning look towards Juan; clearly something is happening on the island, something that must pose a great deal of danger towards me.

'Marcus, I know that you don't approve, but how can you possibly keep her safe if she isn't reprised of all of the facts. Eloise, we have been reliably informed that Eduardo has found a way on to the Island, we believe that one of his many spies has helped and hidden him somewhere. The security detail around you will be bulked out with not only Dalton and Ricardos guards, but also my own.'

I sit back down heavily, the colour draining from my face, the realisation that he is here, that he has come for me filling me with dread. Looking around at our surroundings, trying to find any small space that he could be hidden and watching us, I try to compose myself. Although there are plenty of guards surrounding us, I decide that I would feel a lot safer in my apartment at the main house, away from prying eyes.

'I think I'd like to go back to the main house now, Marcus would you mind taking me?'

Marcus places his hand on my elbow and helps me rise to my feet, guiding me through the house and back to the Jeep. Settling on the back seat, I am surprised when Marcus climbs in next to me. 'Manuel, take it slow please, I need to speak to Eloise.'

Turning slowly to look at me, concerned that I may still be fearful of him, 'Eloise, I'm sorry but, he shouldn't have told you that.'

'What about my father possibly being on the Island? I'm glad he did, at least if I had any stupid thoughts about going off on my own, I now know why it isn't possible.'

'No he shouldn't have told you that if you don't want to marry Dalton you won't have to' looking at me with pity, as he tells me the truth behind my decision, one that could ruin the lives of everyone that I had recently met. 'If you choose not to marry Dalton, you need to be aware of the implications that will arise afterwards; the alliance between your grandfather, Ricardo, and Dalton will be destroyed, which could lead to a war and a lot of people will be killed. We are lucky that we are too young to remember the turbulent times, when all of the families were vying for power over each other, until the alliance was formed. The threat from Eduardo will not diminish; he hates your grandfather as much as he hates Ricardo. Dalton will be left fighting two wars; one against your grandfather, for taking you away from him, and one against your father, in an effort to continue to keep you safe. Whatever you think of him, he is a good man, most of the people under his care owe him their lives, you cannot buy that kind of loyalty. I know that this is a lot for you to take in, but if you really do believe that to make an informed decision you need to know all of the facts, then I feel that I have no choice.'

Pulling up outside Daltons home, my thoughts in overdrive; if I marry Dalton tomorrow, I will continue to be ruled over by him, in his efforts to keep me safe, but, if I choose not to go through with our vows tomorrow I will be to blame for the deaths of hundreds of innocent people; whenever there is a war it is always the innocent who suffer.

As soon as the Jeep comes to a stop, the door is yanked open, Dalton is absolutely furious as he looks into the car. When he sees that I am sat there, perfectly safe, he looks in Marcus' direction, 'Where the hell have you been, Juan phoned when you left, you should have been back ages ago.'

Marcus removes himself from the car and stands in front of Dalton, trying to calm him down, explaining that we were simply having a leisurely drive, rather than telling him of the talk we had had.

As they were both preoccupied, I took it as a sign to make my way back to the apartments.

Without taking his eyes off of Marcus, Daltons hand shot out and wrapped his fingers around my wrist, glancing at me, and with a commanding tone 'wait there.'

Removing my wrist from his grasp, 'I don't think so, when you boys have finished your pissing contest come and find me. I don't need to hear this. As you can see, Marcus has done his job and I am safe.' Before I loose my nerve, I walk into the cool building and head to my apartment, bumping into Sophia on my way.

'Miss, dress on now,' the look of relief on her face tells

me that she is relieved that she has found me, it would appear as if Daltons rage, caused by my late arrival, has been felt throughout the house.

Wonderful, just as I think that I will be able to get some peace and quiet to mull things over, my dress is ready to try on. As I have not yet decided whether or not I will go through with the sham wedding tomorrow, I head to the lounge to try it on.

Walking through the door, everyone looks in my direction; word must have spread that the wedding may be off. Putting on my best smile I walk towards the mannequin in the centre of the room, it has been covered with a sheet, ready for the grand reveal. As the sheet is lifted off, I tell myself that I must at least try to look overjoyed with it, but as soon as the sheet is lifted off of it fully, the joy on my face is real. The dress is absolutely divine; the tight fitting bodice is covered with tiny blue crystals that catch the light of the midday sun, which gradually become more and more sparse as it hits the lace of the halter-neck, the skirt of the dress has small crystals in the same colour dotted all over it. It is absolutely perfect, and I cannot wait to try it on.

Feeling somewhat self-conscious I strip off in front of a room full of complete strangers, whilst they remove the dress from the mannequin. Placing it on the floor I step in to it, Lucia and another assistant pull it over my body and begin to lace up the corset back, adjusting it as they go.

Standing in front of the full-length mirror placed by the windows, allowing the light to hit the gems on my gown, I look and feel like a bride. The workmanship of the gown, completed in less than a day is simply exquisite; I cannot believe what they have accomplished in such a short space of time.

Armed with her tray of pins, Lucia makes the necessary adjustments to make sure that it fits me perfectly; in my eyes the gown looks perfect as it is, but Lucia being the perfectionist continues to pin the gown in place. When she is happy, she stands away and takes in masterpiece that has been created.

Hearing a tap at the window, we all look in the direction it has come from, to see Dalton standing there a smug grin on his face, knowing full well that it is bad luck to see the dress before the big day. Matteo quickly closes the curtain, hoping that he hasn't seen too much, whilst Sophia opens the door and sticks her head outside to find out what it is he wants.

'Senor want to speak to you.'

'Ok, Lucia, would you mind helping me out of the gown please,' staring at my reflection in the gown, I know that I need to make a decision and quickly.

'But you still need to try on the veil and the jewellery that has been made for you,' Lucia is clearly not happy that the fitting has been cut short, but as I have an important decision to make and the fact that Dalton does not like to be kept waiting, I had better go and speak with him and get it over and done with.

'I'm sure if it as lovely as the dress it will be amazing, thank you so much for all of your hard-work,' doing my best to appease Lucia, which thank fully seems to work, I really do not want to be in the centre of an argument between a hot blooded Italian and an even hotter blooded Mexican.

Helping me out of my dress, I put on the clothes that I wore earlier for the meeting with my grandfather, and go in search of Dalton. I find him sitting on the patio next to the pool, a glass of brandy in his hand, with the decanter placed precariously on the table next to him. Approaching him I can smell the fumes coming from the alcohol, his eyes have a glassy expression from the effects of too much alcohol.

'Are you drunk?'

Tipping the glass towards me, inspecting the liquor, he drains the glass and pours himself another generous measure, 'working on it. Do you want one?'

'No thanks,' sitting in the chair next to him, I watch as he drains the glass again, 'is this advisable?'

Pouring himself another glass, he looks at me with eyes filled with sadness, 'Probably not, but it will help numb me from what I know is coming next.'

So this is it, do I marry this complicated man, who through some sense of guilt wants to marry me, or do I leave this evening with my grandfather, knowing that a war will ensue? It's a tough choice, but I cannot allow the blood of innocents be on my hands, knowing that I am the cause of their suffering, and that by simply saying yes, it could have all been avoided. But seeing the state that he has gotten himself into, I decide that I will not make it easy for him.

'I don't understand, what do you think is coming next?'

'Given that you now know who your Grandfather is, and the fact that he can give you the perfect get out clause, and whisk you away from me; you are going to tell me that you will not marry me,' looking away from me he stares at the floor, 'aren't you?'

'I see, and did Marcus tell you about our little chat on the way back?'

'No, I was too angry with him, I was so worried that something had happened to you. Why what did he say?'

'He told me the truth about what would happen if we

didn't go through with this sham tomorrow.'

Looking at me with darkness in his eyes, his anger from earlier quickly rising its head again, 'Don't ever call this marriage a sham.'

'Why? I am simply calling it what it is, you know it and so do I, what is the point in beating around the bush?'

'Regardless of what you think of it, our guests will begin to arrive shortly, I need to know what your decision is. If there is to be no wedding tomorrow, I will need to start contacting people to let them know. What have you decided?'

'Before I decide can you answer me this; if the wedding is cancelled, will your alliance with my grandfather be safe?'

'No, I would not be able to forgive him for taking you away from me.'

'So basically innocent people will suffer if I do not marry you,' holding my hand up to silence him, 'Marcus has already told me that warring between the factions would begin again, you would have to fight these off, possibly go to war with my grandfather to maintain your hierarchy, and still have the oncoming war with my father to deal with. Is this true?'

'In essence, yes, but, to honour you, I would not attack your Grandfather first. Eventually, when all of the factions have fizzled out, it would be inevitable that our two families would go to war, the alliance that has been built would crumble to ash.'

'Then I really have no choice, I will not have the blood of the innocents on my hands.'

'Does this mean that…'

'Yes, I'll marry you.' Resigned to my fate, as I can see no other option but this one, perhaps one day I'll be happy with the decision that I have made today. But I know that I will never be able to have the longed for children with him, we would never be able to keep them safe whilst allowing them enough freedom to grow.

Picking me up from my chair and placing me on his lap, 'you have made me the happiest man alive' kissing me patiently, with lips full of promise for what our future will hold. I can feel his erection prodding into my thigh; I so want to feel him inside of me again, yearning for the ecstasy that only he can give me. But I am also aware that it would be wrong to take advantage of him whilst he is inebriated, his promise of making the wait worth my while, ringing in my ears, removing myself from his grip I stand and make some distance between us.

'Much as I would love to see where this is going to end up, we are getting married tomorrow and it is bad luck for the groom to see the bride the night before the wedding.'

As he reaches for me, I move back slightly further, he growls with annoyance and with his lightening quick reflexes he manages to stand and hold me captive in his arms before I have time to react. His hands are in my hair, forcing his lips onto mine with such urgency that I became fearful he would create bruises to form on them, trying to pull away to lessen the impact of them as his tongue begins it's deep exploration of my mouth, I can taste the brandy on his tongue. Walking me backwards towards the wall of the apartment, with my back against the building and Dalton rock-hard body pressed close to my chest, I am captive, unable to move as his hands begin to search my body aggressively. Sliding his hand into my pants, seeking the soft mound of flesh that gives us both so much pleasure, I try to hold onto something concrete to stop myself slipping into the place where lust rules my mind, and allows me to let him do whatever he likes to my body.

Just as I am about to slip into the place of no return, we hear someone clearing their throat from inside the open door to the apartment. Detaching ourselves from each other and quickly straightening our clothes, Dalton places his finger, wet from my passion, into his mouth, and looking into my eyes he sucks on it suggestively. The lust that creeps into his eyes has a ripple effect on me as I feel my mound pulsate with longing yet again. How on earth can one look have such an effect on me?

'Yes, and this better be good' Dalton is not happy about being interrupted, whereas I am ashamed at how quickly I forgot how many guards are on duty, and are able to see our passion unfurl in front of them.

Marcus steps through the door, a look of amusement on his face, he has obviously seen the little show we were putting on for the spectating guards.

'Boss, there has been another one, he's definitely on the Island.'

Dalton charges into the house, Marcus hot on his heels with me following closely behind. I refuse to be kept in the dark any longer, if it is something pertaining to me, then I have a right to know.

Following the men into his office, Juan and Ricardo have already taken up residence on one of the sofas; a pile of nearly a dozen Polaroid photos are stacked on top of the coffee table. Ignoring their requests to leave, I pick them up, and begin to flick through them; one shows me sitting with my Grandfather on his patio, the others show my movements from this morning; leaving the main house and getting in to the jeep and then from the jeep to my grandfathers house. Considering the distance and timings required to take these pictures, more than one person must have taken them, either that or one of the guards in my security detail is the spy. A shiver goes through me with the realisation that the men who watch over me the most could be relaying information to my father. When I look at the final picture, I instantly release it and drop them all to the floor; the image taken from behind me, shows me standing in front of a full-length mirror dressed in my wedding gown. Someone had been in my apartment, fear and rage makes me begin to shake; someone had been in my apartment and taken a picture to give to my father.

Seeing the colour drain from my face, Dalton places a glass of brandy in my hand and sits me next to him on the sofa, picking up the photos from the floor, he begins to leaf through them, when he sees the one of me in my dress, the rage that is emanating from him is frightening.

'Marcus, have you seen this? They were in her fucking apartment! Gather the men who were on duty this morning and question them, we need to get to the bottom of this.'

Marcus takes the photo from Dalton and I could see the absolute anger form on his face possibly because of the guilt he feels in his part of my abduction, he drops the picture and flies out of the door, shouting out the names of the guards who were part of my detail this morning.

'Dalton, I suggest replacing the guards in charge of Eloise's safety with my own, until we can discover who this person is.'

'Juan, I agree with you, thank you for your offer. Mi pequeno pajaro, I promise we will discover who this person is, and I promise that we will keep you safe, we will not allow your father to hurt you.'

Sitting quietly on the sofa I begin to sip the brandy from the glass that Dalton has given me, it is already having the desired effect and numbing my senses. Feeling vulnerable and knowing Daltons resolve about breaking traditions an idea comes to my mind.

'Can I ask, if Marcella isn't busy, if she would be able to stay with me tonight? I have always found her to be comforting, and I believe that her presence will help me feel safe.'

Ricardo stands, and signals for Juan to follow him, 'yes of course, I'll send for her now.'

'No, I do not want you to send for her, I would like you to ask her if she minds, she is not a possession to be ordered around, she is a human being.'

'So like her mother,' Juan chuckles as they leave the room.

Dalton holds me close, as I finish the amber liquid, he doesn't try to kiss me again, as we both know where this would lead, part of me really wanted so slide on top of him, and tease his cock to life through his trousers; whereas another part of me just wanted to curl up on my bed like a frightened child and shut out the world.

A thought suddenly strikes me, 'when we say our vows tomorrow, will I be called Eloise Mansell or Samira Jade Ramirez?'

'That depends on you, what would you like to be called?'

'Well, for as long as I can remember I have been called Eloise, but as she doesn't really exist, I guess I would like to start my new life with you as Samira, although it may take some time to get used to people calling me that.'

'Samira,' feeling the sound out as it rolls off of his tongue, 'Samira Jade Mercedes, yes I think if fits quite well. You never cease to amaze me, while the world is crashing down around you, your main thought is you name at the time of taking our vows. I love you Samira,' kissing me passionately, making me unable to think about his last statement, but deciding that he has definitely had too much to drink.

A knock at the door breaks us apart, as Marcus sticks his head around, 'the guards have been replaced, and the others have been taken for questioning. It's going to be a long night, are you sure you want to do this now? Your guests will be arriving soon. They can't do any harm if they are locked up, we can start to question them in a couple of days, lack of food and water may loosen their tongues after all.'

The thought of someone being tortured to extract information made me feel sick, deciding that I have heard enough, 'I can't listen to this, I'm going back to the apartment. If Marcella is free and happy to stay with me tonight could someone show her where I am please.'

'Yes of course,' Marcus steps through the door and closes it briefly, 'Eloise, I need to make you aware that on your grandfathers orders you have a serious amount of guards now, he has even requested that they be stationed inside of your bedroom.'

'What? That's completely ridiculous, tell him that it isn't necessary.'

'I have tried, believe me, his response was that he has already lost you mother to your father, and he will not loose you to him as well, especially after he has only just found you. Take my advice and let it go, it is only for one night, I'm sure after tomorrow they won't want to watch you two, you know' raising his eyebrows suggestively, I feel the flush of redness rise in my face, which causes him to laugh at my evident embarrassment.

'Oh my god, Marcus, really? Did you have to say that to her? Come on Samira, I'll take you back to your apartment and away from this potty mouthed fiend.'

The camaraderie between these two men makes me chuckle as we leave the office, my embarrassment soon forgotten. The sight that greeted me made me stop laughing immediately, there are two rows of guards, with ten men on each side, forming a corridor for me to walk through. When I walk towards the centre of them, they closed rank and form a circle around Dalton and myself, their weapons raised, watching for any imminent threats.

'Now this is overkill,' I whisper to Dalton, who simply chuckles next to me. 'Is Marcus still in charge of my security?'

'Yes, he would not relinquish command ma'am,' the guard closest to me informs me.

I couldn't help smiling at Dalton, mouthing the word "ma'am" at him.

When we reach the door leading to the apartment, the guards at the front of the circle filter inside leaving the rest behind us. As we move to step in to the apartment, one of the guards blocks Daltons path.

'Sorry sir, Senor Ramirez has requested that you do not enter the apartment today,' knowing that this will possibly result in a tirade of abuse from Dalton, 'he is a stickler for traditions, you will see your bride at the alter tomorrow.'

'Well how can I argue with an old mans request,' taking me in a gentle embrace, he cups my chin and kiss me full on the lips, 'I will see you tomorrow Samira,' whispering in my ear, 'I can't wait for tomorrow night, it has been too long since I was inside of you.'

Turning on his heel the guards separated as I watch his retreating back, heading towards the kitchens and Magda.

Entering the apartment, I was surprised to see Marcella already here, my excitement at seeing her made me run into her warm embrace, as she smoothed my hair and made shushing noises, I was unaware that the emotions of the day have caused a few tears to leak from my eyes.

'Eloise, or should that be Samira?' Seeing the shocked look on my face at the realisation that she now knows my true identity, she chuckles, 'word spreads fast on this Island, the women at the cabin are overjoyed for your grandfather, that he has found you after all of these years.' Standing back and holding me at arms length, she gives me the once over, 'you look well, I cannot recognise the broken girl who came to me at the cabin. Sophia has made some tea for us, I have been told to make sure that you eat something.'

'Thank you so much for coming, I really appreciate it. I'm feeling so much better now, although slightly apprehensive about tomorrow.'

'Why would you be apprehensive, surely you should be happy, Dalton is quite a catch you know.'

She evidently does not know the real reason behind the wedding, knowing that I can trust her I decide to tell her the truth, 'How much do you know about why we are marrying?'

'Nothing, I would assume that you are both madly in love and cannot wait to get married, either that or you are pregnant and you wish to marry before you begin to show.'

'Sorry to disappoint you but you are wrong on both counts,' seeing her face fall, not understanding why anyone would not marry for love, 'lets have lunch and I can fill you in.'

Marcella follows me to the kitchen where Sophia is in a flap, looking around the room, I soon see the cause to her distress, there are guards stationed in each corner of the room, watching her every move. It would seem that, although Dalton has a great deal of trust in her, my Grandfather has none. Remembering her panic when I discovered that she could actually speak fluent English, I couldn't help wondering if there is something more in her deceit.

'Sophia, sit down, I will see to lunch,'

'No miss, I do, my job,' she continues to move plates of food from the work surfaces to the kitchen table.

Taking the plates from her hands before she is able to deposit them, 'Sophia, sit, I am more than capable of finishing our lunch, please, I will not ask again.' I hate the sound of giving one of my friends an order, but the state that she has gotten herself into, I could see no other way of making her do as I ask.

Sophia sits down with a deflated bump, with her head down; she occasionally glances nervously at the guards. I couldn't understand why their presence would shake her so, since my arrival we have been surrounded by guards; admittedly they have always been on the perimeter of the apartment, so perhaps that is the problem.

Placing the last plate of food on the table, I begin to open the cupboards in search of cups and plates. Once I have found them, I place three plates on the table and attempt to give a plate to each of the guards, 'help yourself to the food if you like.'

One of the guards approaches the table, his mouth

salivating at the prospect of trying some of the delicious food that Sophia has prepared.

'Private, back to your post,' the sound of one of the guards shouting is deafening in the confined space of the kitchen. 'Ma'am, thank you, but we need to be alert to any threats. Please do not distract us, try to pretend that we are not here.'

Looking at the guard that has spoken, I cannot help but wonder how you would pretend that he is not here. He is so imposing, over six foot tall and built like a brick shit house, this man is massive, and I could imagine him going head to head with some of the best body builders in the world, and winning.

'Ok, suit yourself,' turning to the women seated at the table, as they take in the interaction between the guard and myself, Marcella with a slight grin, whilst Sophia looks petrified. 'Coffee or tea?'

They answer in unison, 'coffee please.'

Putting the kettle on to boil, I place a tea bag in one cup and a spoonful of coffee in the other two, I was tempted to offer the soldiers a cup, but I am pretty sure that the officer in charge would put me across his knee for insubordination.

Placing the cups of hot fluid in front of Marcella and Sophia, I squeeze the teabag against the side of the cup before adding milk, and carrying my cup to the table, sitting next to Sophia, and placing my hand over hers in an act of providing comfort to her.

'Right girls, lets tuck in,' reaching for a salmon and cucumber sandwich before taking a bite.

Looking at the Marcella seated opposite me at the table, I notice that although she has picked up a sandwich, she is opening it and inspecting the contents as if fearful that it will poison her.

Chuckling at her reaction as she takes a cautious bite, deciding that she quite likes it and devours the rest in appreciation.

'I take it that you haven't had a Salmon and Cucumber sandwich before?'

'No, I haven't, but it is rather nice.'

'It's a British classic, most coffee shops sell them.' Deciding that that is enough small talk, I begin to tell Marcella the true cause of the upcoming wedding ceremony between Daltons and myself.

Sitting back and pursing her lips, she exhales loudly, 'so let me get this straight; you do not love Dalton?'

'Correct'

'And Dalton does not love you'

'Correct'

'And you are definitely not pregnant'

Smiling to myself as the older woman tries to make sense of everything that I have told her, 'also correct.'

'You are marrying him so that there will not be a war?'

'Pretty much, I would never be able to live with myself if innocent people are hurt or killed because of my actions. At the moment this is the best way to safeguard their wellbeing.'

'So what happens in the future, when all of the threats have disappeared? Eventually your Grandfather will die and you will be left in charge of his empire'

Realising that she is speaking the truth, my Grandfather is indeed elderly, and being his only living heir I stand to inherit his fortunes, answering as honestly as I can, 'I don't know, I haven't given it any thought, I suppose that we will cross that bridge when we come it.'

I watch as Marcela rises from the table, crossing to me

she embraces me in a tight hold, whispering in my ear, 'thank you for your selflessness, you do not know how many people that your actions will be saving.'

I spend the rest of the afternoon, relaxing by the pool, the guards are never far from my side, affording me little privacy, I can hear Marcella and Sophia talking frantically in the background, but as they are speaking in their native tongue, I can make little sense of what is being said.

After joining the women for dinner, which I spend most of the time pushing the food around my plate, the nerves from overthinking my decision making it impossible to eat.

'Samira, please eat something, you will need your energy for tomorrow' the concern showing on Marcellas face as she watches me plays thoughtfully with my food.

'I'm sorry I just can't eat anything, nerves have got the best of me.'

Rising from the table, I excuse myself and retire to my room. I had always thought of this space as the only place I could get some privacy, but on entering I see that there are indeed guards stationed inside of my room, two on every door, and one in each corner making at least ten guards. Sighing with resentment at having my personal space invaded, I cross the room and enter the bathroom, turning the taps on I watch as the bath begins to fill, absentmindedly mixing the hot and cold water with my hands. Is this going to be my life now? Married to Dalton Mercedes, my every move monitored by heavily armed men. Or will they decide that as soon as we have exchanged our vows I will be afforded some privacy?

Stepping into the too hot water, I stand naked in the bath, waiting for my skin to become accustomed to the temperature, before sitting down and laying with my head propped on the back of the bath. I'm getting married in the morning, the thought that my life has changed so dramatically in such a short space of time, was overwhelming. I begin to sob silently, hoping that the guards will not hear me, with the realisation that as soon as I have said my vows, I will never be free. He has held me captive in mind and body since the moment we have met.

A small tap at the door breaks me from my thoughts; Marcella is standing at the other side of door 'Samira, can I come in please' without waiting for me to answer, the door is pushed open, and Marcella walks slowly in to the room. 'You left so abruptly, that I wanted to check if you are ok? Oh, my dear, why the tears? Everything will be ok, given time you may even find yourself being happy being married to Dalton; he will care for you and protect you like no other.'

'I know, but I feel trapped, whichever decision I make someone will get hurt. I feel as if I am sacrificing myself for the good of others; people that I do not even know. I will be fine, don't worry, I am just overthinking things.'

Concern showing on her face at my resignation to my fate, 'Come on, lets get you in to bed, Sophia is making up a bed for me next to yours, we decided that it may distract the guards if we were to share again.'

The thought of the guards being distracted by two women sharing a bed made me begin to laugh, and once I had started I could not stop, tears streaming down my face as I step out of the bath and gratefully take the towel from Marcellas hands.

Dressed in a satin negligee, I climb into my bed, Marcella places the covers over me, lay on top of the covers next to me, she runs her hands soothingly over my hair and begins to hum me softly to sleep.

NINE

Waking the next morning to the sound of birdsong coming through the open doors, I stretch, feeling rested from a good nights sleep. Looking at the empty bed next to me, I see that Marcella has already risen; I can hear her in the kitchen, humming loudly to herself. The thought that today is my wedding day springs to my mind. Swinging my legs out of the bed, I walk towards the en-suite to have a shower, thinking to myself that we may as well get this show on the road.

Hearing Marcella crash through the bedroom door with a tray of pastries and freshly squeezed orange juice, I stick my head around the door, 'I'll be out in a minute I am just going to have a quick shower.'

'I have breakfast for you, come and eat first.'

Looking at the tray of sweet pastries, my stomach begins to complain with hunger, but know that the nerves that I am feeling will not allow me to keep anything down yet, 'I honestly couldn't eat anything, even if I wanted to, sorry.'

'Ok, but you will promise me that you will eat something at the wedding breakfast, after you have exchanged your vows, Dalton will be cross with me if he discovers that you haven't eaten.'

'Yes, of course, I promise, thank you for not telling him.'

Leaving the room with the tray, Marcella shoots over her

shoulder, 'hurry with your shower, the make up artist and hairdresser will be arriving soon. I will come and get you in five minutes.'

Stepping into the shower, I lather up the shampoo in my hair, rinsing it of before beginning to wash my body, thinking to myself that for a sham wedding they have certainly pushed the boat out; a make up artist and a hairdresser, along with the handmade gown and jewellery, a definite example of extravagance.

Stepping out of the shower as I hear Marcella enter the bedroom, the excitement of the upcoming wedding has suddenly hit her. The normally unflappable woman is now in full flap mode, pushing me towards the lounge where I find a hairdressers station set up alongside one for the make up artist.

Taking the seat that was pulled out in front of the makeup artist, she begins to shape my nails whilst the hairdresser is behind me, trying to tame my long locks into submission. I feel like a piece of cattle, being primped and preened for market, as these two women do everything they can to make me look glamorous enough to become the wife of Dalton Mercedes.

When they are satisfied that they have done everything required of them, Marcella coos about how beautiful I look. Leading me to Lucia and Matteo, who are patiently waiting to help me into my gown. As I step in to it, they pull it up at either side, and begin to lace the corset back, adjusting the lace at the shoulders so that it sits flat against my body. Matteo supports my arm as I lift a foot for Lucia to slide an elegant satin shoe on each one. The cathedral veil and tiara are secured onto the top of my head with bobby pins, feeling the weight of it I wondered how long I would have to wear it for. If I had to wear it all day, I am sure that it would cause compression of my spine.

With the jewellery added to my outfit and a bouquet of flowers placed in my hands, I watch as the five people in the room stand back to take in my appearance, they all seem really pleased with their hard work. Looking at a very teary Marcella I give her my best smile and hold out my hand to her, giving her a quick squeeze as she takes it.

Matteo moves the only mirror in the room in to my line of vision and then with a flourish and a 'Voila' he removes the white sheet, the movement reminding me of a matador in a bull rink.

Looking at myself in the mirror for the first time wearing the completed outfit, I did a double take, hardly able to believe that I am the person looking back at me. My hair has been teased into a messy up do, with ringlets coming down from my temples. The tiara is exquisite, the gems matching that of my dress and the rest of the jewellery I am wearing; the necklace stopping just shy of my ample cleavage. The dress itself fits perfectly; and it feels like a second skin, the veil reaches beyond the hem of the dress at the back, and edged with lace that matches the dress, the light coming through the glass doors picking out the minute gemstones that have been hand stitched to it. The bouquet consisted of white lilies, interspersed with black and blue roses. I looked like a bride, full of dreams for the future life awaiting me, if only the outside world knew of the torment that I am feeling right now.

'Samira, you look beautiful my child,' looking in the direction of the voice, I see my grandfather walking towards me, his arms outstretched as he takes me in a tight embrace. Releasing me he looks down at my face, a tear in his eyes, 'you remind me of your mother so much, I wish she could be here to see this day.'

Holding the old mans hands I give them a quick squeeze, 'I know, me too.'

'El … I mean Samira, sorry that is going to take some getting used to; it's time to go,' Marcus is standing at the door looking flushed that he almost slipped up.

'Eloise is fine, honestly, I don't mind, it will take some getting used to for me as well. Lead the way, Marcus.'

'Ah, I can't stay with you, Dalton has made me his best man,' the smile of pride that spreads across his face was so nice to see, he always seems so stern and unapproachable. 'I need to tell you that there has been a change of plan on the venue, you will no longer be married in the chapel, we decided that there were too many places that couldn't be guarded sufficiently along the route, so you will now be married in the grounds here.'

'Right, ok, lets get this show on the road then.'

Leaning down, he takes my hands in his, with a sly smile on his face he gives me a quick peck on the cheek, 'don't tell Dalton I did that, or he'll kick my arse.' Laughing as he retreats to take his place as best man, I can't help but chuckle about how at ease he is with the whole situation.

My grandfather and I watch as everyone, except for the guards, vacate the room, as they take their places for the ceremony.

Placing my hand in his, we walk towards the grounds at the back of the mansion; the band strikes up the wedding march as they see us approach.

Walking down the makeshift aisle, with our guests seated either side, who turn to watch me approaching Dalton standing in front of Padre Marcellous, with Marcus by his side; I try to shut out their looks of disapproval. It is clear to see that they are not happy with our union, especially as it steals their last hope of using me to exact revenge towards my father.

I could not have chosen the setting any better if I had tried; Magda has done a truly wonderful job of organising our wedding. The rows of white chairs are adorned with blue sashes, with a bouquet of blue flowers on the end of each row.

Looking at Dalton, dressed immaculately in a pure white tuxedo, standing beneath the long tendrils of a weeping willow, my heart flutters with nervous anticipation. Although I know that I do not have any choice in going through with this marriage as too many people stand to be hurt if I do not, the feeling of doubt and apprehension continues to spread through me.

Perhaps Dalton is feeling the same as he refuses to turn to look at me approaching him. Marcus on the other hand looks over his shoulder winking at me, whilst jabbing Dalton playfully in the ribs.

Seeing this playful interaction between the two men makes me smile, my nerves quickly forgotten.

My grandfather kisses me quickly on my cheek and releases my hand, placing it in Daltons, who quickly glances out of the corner of his eye at me. Squeezing my hand slightly, confirming that I am standing next to him and that it isn't a figment of his imagination.

Padre Marcellous clears his throat to silence the congregation who are witnessing this sham, before beginning the ceremony.

As if living in a dream state we recite our vows word for word, and Dalton places a wedding band on my ring finger.

Looking down at the simple platinum ring, I realise that that is it, we are now married and I have become Mrs Dalton Mercedes, now I am truly trapped; but at least with my self-sacrifice I have potentially saved the lives of innocent victims.

'I now pronounce you man and wife, you may kiss the bride,' the Padre says with pride.

Dalton finally turns to look at me full on, the look of pride and lust on his face sends shivers direct to my core, which begins to pulsate with longing. Placing his hands carefully on my waist he pulls me close and places a deep kiss on my lips, the sparks fly instantly and I can feel his arousal pressing up against me. Hearing the cheers and whoops of congratulations from the spectators I break the kiss. I instantly regret severing the contact with him as my need and lust is so powerful for him, although I am sure that our guests do not want ringside seats at the consummation of our marriage, the look in Daltons eyes tells me that he really couldn't care who is there watching us, the lust he feels a mirror image of my own.

Taking me by the hand, he leads me down the aisle at the sound of the cheers and applause from our guests, an occasional slap on his back as he passes some of the men. So much rice and confetti is being thrown over us that it makes it difficult for us to see the path in front of us.

Dalton pulls me into an empty room, and closes the door behind me slamming my back against the door, his hands frantically searching my body, pulling the dress of my skirt up, and pushing my pants to one side, he plunges his fingers forcefully inside of me, the mixture of pleasure and pain, from being stretched so quickly, make me beg him to stop.

'I want you so badly, I cannot control myself, you are

mine now, I can do what ever I like with you, you belong to me, I own you.'

'Dalton stop, please, our guests are waiting for us.'

'I do not care, I want your body wrapped around my cock as I slam it into you, I have waited too long to hear you scream my name with ecstasy.'

If I am honest with myself, right here in this moment, I wanted nothing more, but hearing our guests moving in the corridor behind the closed door, brought me to my senses. An idea begins to form, which may help alleviate the lust he is compounded to release.

Reaching for his fly, I unzip it, and place my hand inside, beginning to massage along the length of his hard member. Removing his fingers from inside of me, and forcing me to my knees, I come face to face with the bulging tip of his penis, taking hold of it tentatively; I carefully close my lips around it, firstly because I was afraid of hurting him, and secondly I have never done this voluntarily before, and I am unsure if I am doing it correctly. Gradually inserting him into my mouth, just before I hit my gag reflex I remove it just as slowly. Dalton moans in delight at the slow movements I am making, but he quickly becomes impatient with how slow I am going, and holding my face in his hands, he begins to thrust deeper and harder into my mouth. Hitting the back of my throat with every thrust; and causing me to gag, which leaves me struggling to draw breath. I say a silent prayer, hoping for this to be over soon, my little brainwave did not take into account Daltons desire to fuck hard, neither did it include this assault. As if the gods are listening, my prayers are swiftly answered, as I feel him begin to swell and hot semen hits the back of my throat. I quickly swallow the contents of my mouth, cautious that none of it should spill on my pristine white dress.

Kneeling on the floor, trying to make sense of what just happened, I watch as Dalton tucks himself back inside, pulling up the fly on his trousers and adjusting his shirt.

Helping me to my feet, he kisses me, 'you are amazing; I cannot wait until I can fuck you later. I may even have to ask our guests to leave early.'

Whilst I also cannot wait until later, the sense of dread invading me makes me worry that since taking our vows, his sexual appetite and deviances will come into play. Especially as he now thinks that he owns me, but as far as I am aware, a marriage certificate is not a purchase order.

Fixing our appearances, Dalton leads me to our waiting guests in the Dining room; where I see that Magda has out done herself with the buffet she has prepared. Alongside the traditional Mexican dishes, she has made some English ones for me. I notice that she has already cut and prepared the scones, laden with cream and strawberry jam, looking at Dalton, he confirms.

'My father insisted that they be prepared properly, he didn't think the cleaners would appreciate cleaning up the crumbs from our guests spitting them out.'

His mood has definitely changed, his orgasm making him more upbeat and less wound up.

Mingling with our guests, Dalton stays a permanent fixture at my side, introducing each person to me whilst tracing small circles on the exposed flesh of my back, the shock waves it creates make it difficult to think let alone speak.

The look of distaste does not leave the faces of our guests, looking around the room I realise that most of the people gathered would like to inflict great harm on me. These are dangerous people, and for the first time since my arrival I am truly thankful for the armed guards who are forever within easy reach of me. Although Dalton has assured me that these people will not harm me whilst we are married, I am certain that they are assessing our interaction for any chinks in the armour of our relationship, which they can utilise for their own ends.

Throughout the reception Dalton continues to make sure that my glass is permanently topped up, knowing that he is aware that I am not a big drinker I look at him questioningly, wondering what his end game is. He simply returns the look with a boyish grin, tipping the glass towards my lips and making me drink the rest of the contents.

Signalling to Marcus, who approaches quickly, Dalton whispers in his ear, before he departs just as quickly. I look questioningly at Dalton, but whatever was said between the men, one look tells me that he isn't about to divulge it.

Tapping a knife against the side of his glass, all of our guests become silent and look towards the origin of the noise, 'Ladies and Gentlemen, on behalf of my beautiful bride and myself, I would like to thank you for coming and helping to celebrate our wedding with us. However, it would appear that the excitement of the day has gone straight to Samiras head, so we will retire. Please feel free to stay for as long as you wish, there is plenty of food and drink available, and if you need anything else, please feel free to ask one of the staff.'

On a rapturous applause and shouts of "congratulations", Daltons pulls me out of the room and leads me upstairs, away from the sounds of our guests enjoying themselves.

'Where are we going, the apartment is that way.'

'We are staying in my room tonight, it is the farthest away we can be from the guests, and the least overlooked place in the house, we should be safe from interruption and prying eyes here.'

As we enter the room, Marcus steps out from inside, taking in my inebriated state he shoots Dalton a warning look.

'It's all clear boss, be careful with her.'

'Thanks Marcus, don't worry I will be. I have worked to hard to protect her to hurt her now. Go back to the party and enjoy yourself, keep some guards stationed at the end of the hall and the stairs. We'll begin the questioning of the guards tomorrow when everyone has left.'

Kicking the door closed behind us, he turns to me with a dark look in his eyes, I can see that his Demons are on full display; he is no longer trying to hide them from me. A shiver of anticipation rocks my body as he hungrily grabs me and rips the dress off of my body.

'Dalton, that dress cost a fortune, what on earth are you doing.'

'The dress means nothing to me, I will have another made for you if you wish to keep hold of it for sentimental reasons. I have waited too long to hear my name on your lips, I'll warn you now that I need to fuck you harder than I have before to pacify my demons, then I will make love to you like no other.'

Dragging me to the bed and throwing me on top of it, he has removed his clothes before I am able to understand the impact of his lust for me, or allowing the fear from his warning to creep into my thoughts.

Pulling me so that my backside is in line with the edge of the bed, he thrusts his cock so deep into me I can feel his balls slapping against my arse. The pain that I feel, as he pile drives me into the bed is so intense I scream out begging for him to stop, trying to move up the bed and away from him. The look in his eyes is so dark, it is like nothing I have seen before, I now know that he has previously kept some of his demons at bay, but here they are in full control of him. The expression on his face telling me that my pleas have fallen on deaf ears. Holding onto me as he continues his relentless thrusting, the fear I am feeling stops the sense of pleasure that I normally have when he invades my body; all I can feel is the pain as if I am being ripped in two.

Trying to squirm out of his grasp, desperate to reach beyond his demons and pull him back to me, I hold his face in my hands, trying to force him to look at me and at the pain that his need is currently causing. Desperately trying to break the spell he is under, as he continues to slam into me over and over. I can feel a bruise forming on my pelvis from the constant colliding action of our bodies.

Releasing my thighs, a small part of me hopes that I have managed to reach him; removing my hands from his face he manoeuvres me into the centre of the bed. Reaching above my head I feel him place a leather restraint around each wrist, securing them tightly and making me immobile, as he pulls me down the bed so that my arms are stretched above my head. All I can do is lay there, hoping that the punishment will soon end, and that his demons will be sated, so that he will come back to me.

He continues thrusting into me with such force, and the pain becomes so intense that I begin to scream in agony, with tears running down my face.

What feels like a lifetime later I feel him begin to swell

inside of me, I know that his release is coming fast, and in an attempt to make the torture end quicker I begin to move my hips towards his thrusting cock, matching his pace until I feel his semen emptying inside of me, the guttural noise coming from deep within him as he empties himself inside of me.

I watch his features as he slowly returns to me, his demons placated and safely hidden away again. Looking down at me, and the tears of agony running down my face, he reaches above my head for the clasp of the restraints to release me. In my mind I know that the second he releases me I am going to bolt for the relative safety of the en-suite, although I know that it is a feeble plan, as if her really wanted to gain entry, there is little I can do to stop him. As if reading my mind, he pauses and looks into my eyes, seeing for the first time the pain and fear deep within them.

'I am sorry if I hurt you, I shouldn't have made us wait so long, I promise that I will be more gentle with you from now on. But I cannot release you; for I know that if I do, you will run away from me. Let me show you how I wanted this evening to go.'

Placing feather light kisses on my tear stained eyes, in an attempt to kiss away the pain that he has caused, he begins to trail kisses down my neck. Pausing at the sensitive flesh at my collarbone, he begins to nibble gently at it, causing a stirring of desire deep below. I am amazed at how quickly this complicated man can awaken the hidden desires within me.

Continuing his trail of kisses moving south, he finds the soft mounds of my breasts and begins to playfully tease with my nipples, causing them to rise into stiff peaks, I can feel the arousal that this causes in him, and I hold my breath, waiting for his usual practice of inflicting a small amount of pain along with a great deal of pleasure.

Cupping my sensitive mound of flesh in his hands, he begins to gently rub at the cluster of nerves of my clitoris, causing me to arch my back. Placing three fingers deep inside of me, the pain from his violent fucking quickly forgotten, as my body begins to open up to him. With slow teasing strokes, he slides his fingers inside of me, flexing them and hitting my g-spot as he removes them, then slowly sliding them inside of me again, I can feel his knuckles inside of me as they enter me, making my flesh envelope around them.

Releasing my nipple from his mouth, he continues to trail a line of kisses towards the parting at the top of my thighs. Taking my swollen clitoris in to his mouth, he begins to suck gently on it, twirling his tongue around the sensitive organ, shock waves of pleasure ripple through me. I find myself thrusting my pelvis into his face, begging for him to fuck me harder and deeper.

Feeling a pressure on my sphincter, I know what is coming next, eager anticipation makes me crave the final assault on my senses, stretching me to my limits.

Slowly sliding a finger inside my anus, I can feel my body tightening as an orgasm approaches. He continues his slow assault with his hands, his mouth continuing to suck and twirl around my clitoris. The tension building inside of me makes me plead with him to fuck me harder and make me cum, desperate for the final release. Again my pleas fall on deaf ears, as he refuses to change the pace and give me what I so desperately need.

Gradually I feel the tension in my body leave as a

powerful orgasm rocks it, the growling noise coming from deep within me sounding so alien to me. Dalton stops suckling on my now very sensitive clitoris and rising to his knees he looks down at me, his hands continue their assault on me, causing another earth shattering orgasm to swiftly come.

Removing his fingers from my sensitive flesh, he stands and walks into his dressing room. When I hear his soft footsteps coming back to the bed, I look up, curious as to what he has in his hands.

Holding up several black phallic looking objects he explains to me, 'I would very much like to fuck your arse very soon, but you are so tight so we need to take the time to train you up first. We will start with this small one, and gradually work our way up to the largest until you have been stretched enough so that I can slide my cock inside of you.'

What he is planning sounds like it will be extremely painful, so I try to squirm up the bed away from him. Although so far he has inserted his finger, these objects look significantly larger, although no as large as his cock. As he flips me over and pulls my arse into the air, all reasoning is gone as I feel him slide his finger slowly into my arse, with careful strokes he begins to slowly thrust into me. The gently action of this movement makes me begin to purr, he slowly pushes his cock through the soft folds of my wet tunnel. I can feel the tip of his engorged cock as the folds of my skin allow him deeper access. I feel my anus being stretched even further as he inserts a second finger, continuing his slow thrusting with his cock; I feel an orgasm begin to take hold of me. He slowly teases it out of me with his slow deep thrusting.

Removing his fingers from my anus I feel the smallest

black object being pushed slowly into my arse. I can feel myself slowly being stretched even more, the feeling is slightly painful as the widest part is pushed inside of me, my sphincter closing around the end, keeping it in place. Dalton slowly begins to tease my opening with my fingers, the anticipation making my breath come in deep gasps. Carefully placing his fingers inside of me, he slowly teases another orgasm from me.

When he is satisfied that I have become accustomed to the smallest one, I wait for him to remove it, ready to insert the next sized one. To my surprise and satisfaction, I feel his cock slowly seeking entrance to my vagina, which was soon given. He slowly removes his cock and toy, and just as slowly inserts them again; the sensation of being completely filled and stretched had me tightening around his cock as another explosive orgasm rocks my body. Showing no signs of an imminent climax he continues his slow assault of me.

Riding on the waves of yet another powerful orgasm, I do not even feel when he reaches for the next butt plug, pushing it slowly inside of me. The feeling of being stretched even more causes a change in him; he grips my hips painfully, forcing me back on to his cock as the pace of his thrusting increases, his climax is quick to come, as he spurts hot semen inside of me his pace slows down again.

Without giving me time to catch my breath, he inserts the largest of the toys into me, the pain that it causes has me screaming out, ignoring my pleas to stop yet again. He slowly pushes it inside of me, and slowly pulls it out again, gradually my body becomes accustomed to it's length and girth, and the waves of pleasure start to swirl around my body, I feel his cock seeking entrance yet again, and he begins to slide it slowly inside of me. One thrust was all it took for me to cum in the most powerful orgasm yet, my heart is beating rapidly as I take large gasps of fresh air, I can see spots floating on the inside of my eyelids as the tension from my body is released on a tidal wave of pleasure, crashing around me as I sink onto the bed.

Dalton flips me back over, and with the butt plug still firmly lodged inside of me, he slowly slides his cock inside. Supporting his weight on top of me, he begins to kiss me deeply, his tongue rolling around inside of my mouth, exploring every part of it. Ever so slowly, he begins to make love to me, kissing me gently, while the pace of his thrusting penis is so slow, I can feel the fold of my flesh give way to him, before enveloping him completely.

Raising himself above me, he looks into my eyes as he increases the pace and depth of his thrusting, watching me as cum and allowing me to watch him as he climaxes shortly afterwards. Staring intently into one another's eyes as the waves of ecstasy wash over us, is so intense, my heart skips a beat at the love I see in his eyes, a love that I am unsure if I am able to return.

Reaching down, he removes the butt plug, releasing me from the wrist restraints he collapses on top of me, placing a small kiss on my mouth, 'I should have told you this a long time ago, and for taking so long, I can only apologise,' looking into my eyes with such longing, 'Samira Jade Mercedes, I love you.'

Seeing that I am unable to reply in unison, he slides his body off of me and lies next to me, feeling his body relax I can tell that he is fast asleep, with his leg and arm pinning me to the bed.

* * *

Standing on the steps at the front of the house the following morning, encased in Daltons protective arms, we wave farewell to our last guests. A lot of them looking worse for wear, after taking full advantage of Daltons hospitality and partying all night.

Marcus' shouts from inside the house put the guards on high alert as they begin to surround me, with their weapons raised; I was hoping that after yesterdays ceremony the guard detail would be relaxed, but so far it hasn't been. Thoughts of escape are long gone now; especially after discovering my fathers true intent towards me.

I guess one good thing that has come out of yesterdays sham, is that the only threat against me now comes from one person, as the other factions have pulled into line. Their thoughts of using me for revenge placed on the back burner, for now at least. However, if our marriage was to fail, there is no guarantee that their thoughts and plans wouldn't surface again.

Dalton looks around the area, panic-stricken and pulls me inside the relative safety of the cool interior, the guards following suit.

Marcus meets us in the hallway using a white towel to wipe blood off of his hands. His knuckles are swollen, but I cannot see any obvious reason for the blood.

Holding me close to him, Dalton looks at Marcus, 'Well?'

Marcus flashes me with a grim smile, 'he'll start talking soon, but he has requested that he speaks with you.'

'Right, let's go and loosen his tongue.' Holding me tight by his side I have no choice but to walk with him towards the back of the house.

Marcus stops us as we approach a padlocked door, 'boss,

I don't think you should take her down there.'

'She stays, she needs to see what happens to people that betray us.'

Looking between Marcus and Dalton, I can tell that there is a real conflict of interest between them, their roles appearing to be swapped; Marcus has now taken the role of trying to protect me from the horrors of human nature, whilst Dalton is launching me head first into hell.

Marcus opens the door wide for me, as Dalton pushes me towards the opening. There are small lights flickering in holes cut into the concrete walls, the concrete steps, leading down, are gritty beneath my feet. Despite the low lighting it is so dark it that takes a while for my eyes to adjust, feeling the wall tentatively either side of me as we continue to head into the depths of hell. The feelings of oppression and despair, and the smell of blood and fresh urine as we approach the bottom of the steep staircase remind me of a medieval torture chamber, the smell making me urge whilst I try desperately not to empty my stomach contents on the floor.

A sense of doom engulfs me as I hear the cries of the men chained to the walls in the basement. A man is sitting on a chair in the centre of the room; he is completely naked, with his hands bound behind his back and his feet are tied to the chair, I can see the rope burns forming on his wrists and ankles in his frantic efforts to release himself.

Hearing our entrance, the man looks directly at me, ignoring the presence of everyone else in the room.

Spitting blood in my direction, he screams, 'La Puta!'

The hatred that this man still feels for me fills me with fear, how many of the other guards feel the same way? Whilst they have sworn to be loyal to Dalton, they have made no such declaration towards me.

Dalton, glides angrily towards the man, the voice that leaves his mouth is so full of anger that I do not recognise it, 'you dare to disrespect my wife.' His need to protect me from the horrors of the world are quickly forgotten as he holds the man around the throat with one hand and lifts him, chair and all, so that their eyes meet.

The fear this causes in the other man makes him urinate, splashes of it hit Daltons immaculate white trousers and white leather shoes. Looking down at the mess the man has created, he launches him away from him. He lands with a thud, the back of his skull hitting the hard concrete floor, I watch in horror as his lifeless eyes roll back in his head, knowing that Dalton has killed him. Looking down at the lifeless body he shows no empathy, only contempt that the man dared to die before revealing his information.

If I was to ever be asked who I was more afraid of in the entire world, in this moment, right now, I would tell them that Dalton Mercedes scares me the most. The power emanating from him exceeds any anger that I have previously seen. If this is how he rules his world, I want nothing further to do with it, or him.

Moving towards the stairs, my feet shuffling on the loose concrete floor, Dalton looks up from the lifeless man at his feet. Seeing my wish to retreat away from this manmade hell, to be in the light again, he moves towards me. Shrinking back, I hit the hard mass of Marcus' frame, he places his hands comfortingly on my shoulders, but with the fear I now have of my husband I cannot feel them.

Grabbing me by the waist, I am in his arms; his lips

smashing against mine with such force our teeth collide. I can feel the erection protruding towards me, the smell of fear, and blood, and urine, having an aphrodisiac effect on him.

Finally releasing me, he looks down at the broken figure on the floor, 'get him out of my sight.'

I watch with horror as the man is unceremoniously dragged and dumped in the corner of the room.

Rubbing his hands together with glee, he looks at the chained men who have involuntarily wet themselves at seeing Daltons violent outburst, 'so who is next?' Pointing to one of them, 'you, get him down.'

The man pleads with him as he is removed from his shackles, only to be replaced with the ropes on the dead mans chair. 'Boss, please, I don't know anything. Please I beg of you, don't. Mistress,' looking in my direction for help, which I am unable to give, 'please help me, I swear I don't know anything.'

His pleas are quickly silenced as Dalton begins to punch him repeatedly around the face with all of his might.

I feel the blood of the man hitting my face, feeling the warm liquid coagulating on me, breaks me out of my trance. Looking at Marcus standing next to me, I move towards the stairs, 'I cannot watch this. He is an animal, I cannot stay.'

Marcus shrugs his shoulders, and lets me leave, 'where will you be? He will come looking for you.'

'I'll be with Sophia and Marcella in the apartment, I have nowhere else to go.'

Leaving the dankness of the basement I enter the light of the house, it is as if I have left hell and entered heaven.

Pausing at the bathroom in the hallway, I quickly freshen up, scrubbing furiously at the blood on my face, trying to remove all evidence. Knowing that they will ask questions if they see any sign of it, and that at the moment I am not able to put into words what I have just witnessed.

I walk through the apartment door, and find Sophia and Marcella in deep conversation. So intent were they on the conversation that they are having, they do not hear me approach them, my simple greeting makes them jump out of their skins, 'morning ladies.'

Marcella rises from her seat and engulfs me in a maternal hug, 'Samira, you look different, is everything ok?'

'Um, yes, I'm fine, what do you mean I look different?' Shit, does the torture I have witnessed show on my face.

'No, something has changed, I have seen this before, stay here, I need to get something' I watch as Marcella darts out of the apartment, clueless as to what she could possibly mean.

'Miss, I make you coffee, yes?'

'Thank you Sophia, that would be lovely. Do you have time to sit with me and keep me company today? Dalton is doing whatever it is that Dalton does,' worried that I may be caught out on a lie, and made to vocalise the horrors of the basement, I refuse to look in Sophias direction.

'Of course, miss, I get coffee now' Sophia walks towards the kitchen; whilst I sit and watch as the gulls take flight on the sea breeze, thinking about the way Dalton was with me last night, telling me that he loved me, whilst knowing full well that I couldn't reciprocate.

Hearing Sophia walk towards me, the coffee cups clanking on their saucers as she walks, I look towards her as she offers me one of the cups. As soon as the smell hits my nostrils, I can feel the bile threatening to makes its exit. Placing the cup on the table, I cover my mouth and run to the bathroom, getting there just in time as I begin to retch into the toilet.

When I have finished, I stand up and splash cold water over my face, turning I can see Sophia and Marcella watching me with concern on their faces.

'Miss, you ok?'

'I'm fine Sophia, just a little too much champagne yesterday. I'll be with you both soon, I just need a minute ok,' I watch as Sophia turns away and heads back towards the lounge, Marcella however, holds her ground, her gaze running over my body assessing how I look. "Marcella, honestly I'm fine.'

'You are pregnant.' It isn't a question; it is a statement of fact, so sure is she of my condition,

'what? Don't be absurd, if I were pregnant I would certainly know about it.'

'I have something for you, it is your choice if you do it or not, but the sooner you discover the truth the better it will be for the health of your baby,' placing a pregnancy test on the side of the sink

'Marcella, I am not pregnant, will you stop saying such things.'

'Do the test; I will stay with you if you wish. If you are pregnant, then you will have to tell Senor Mercedes, keeping it from him will not be wise.'

Could I be pregnant? Considering that we hadn't used any form of contraception once since we have met, the possibility is entirely plausible. Remembering how rough Dalton was initially with me last night, could he have damaged the baby if I am indeed pregnant? Deciding that knowing the truth would give me all of the information I would need to deal with my future, I reach cautiously for the test. Marcella turns her back as I wee on the tip, and takes it from me when I place the top back over it, placing it next to the sink, we both watch as two faint lines appear in the window, confirming that I am pregnant.

The colour drains from my face as the realisation that I am pregnant sinks in, Marcella holds me close as I sob tears of sorrow for the life that is growing inside of me. How can I bring a child into this life? Putting aside the fact that I just witnessed my husband kill a man with his bare hands, I am virtually a prisoner here, and guarded twenty-four hours a day in an effort to keep me safe from a madman.

'Sssshhhh, it will be ok, you must tell Dalton, it is important that he knows.'

Composing myself, knowing that eventually he will find out when I begin to show, and that the lust he feels for me could damage his child growing inside of me; if I do not tell him, he will be furious at my deception, but if I do tell him, will he be just as furious?

'I know, I will tell him this evening. He will be so angry with me' fearing that he will reject me when he discovers that I am pregnant with his child, admittedly we have never broached the subject of starting a family, but I was sure that he would not be happy about an unplanned pregnancy on top of everything else that is going on.

'My child, of course he won't be angry with you, he is as much to blame as you.'

Hearing a scuffle behind us in the hallway, I see a large shadow as an object is brought down, striking Marcella on the head and she collapses in a heap on the bathroom floor. In the distance I can hear a woman screaming, which is quickly silenced as my father enters the room and strikes me around the face knocking me unconscious.

In the basement, Dalton and Marcus hear one name on the lips of Daltons current victim. Unable to believe, that the person they had given the most trust to with my safety is actually the spy.

Collecting their guns from the locked desk drawer they run full pace towards the apartment, hoping that they are wrong, and that I am safe.

Hearing my screams, Dalton crashes full force through the apartment door, seeing the furniture in disarray and my Grandfathers guards lying in pools of their own blood. He automatically thinks the worse, and begins to search the apartment for my body.

'Samira, where are you' shouting frantically for me.

Marcus finds Marcellas crumpled form in the bathroom, 'Dalton, over here.'

As Marcella begins to rouse from being knocked unconscious, it takes a second for her eyes to focus on the men's faces in front of her.

'Marcella, where is Samira? Where is my wife?'

'I do not know, someone attacked me from behind'

'Boss, you need to see this,' Marcus hands a Polaroid picture to Dalton, of a bound and gagged Samira, with Eduardo and Sophia posing next to her unconscious body. Marcus sees the pregnancy test on the counter and picks it up, seeing the two clear blue lines, he shows it to Dalton, 'it gets worse, she's pregnant.'

Dalton screams in pain and falls to his knees, unable to believe that after all of this time spent trying to keep Samira safe, they realise too late that Sophia is the spy.

Spanish to English

La Puta - Bitch

Pequena ave - Little Bird

el senor quiere que la mires - The Lord wants you to look at her

'Quien es ella?' -'Who is she?'

'No lo se, su nombre es Eloise - 'I don't know, her name is Eloise

English to Spanish

Bitch - La Puta

Little Bird - Pequena ave

The Lord wants you to look at her -el senor quiere que la mires

'Who is she?' - 'Quien es ella?'

'I don't know, her name is Eloise - 'No lo se, su nombre es Eloise

Printed in Great Britain
by Amazon